SUCKER PUNCHED

Clint's fingers had just started to close around the man's wrist when the man pulled his arm back. A jolt of strength along with a quick twist was all he needed to break free of Clint's grasp. Baring his teeth while letting out a snarling breath, the man balled up his fist and sent that same arm straight back at Clint's face.

Although he saw the punch coming, Clint was too close to do much about it and caught the fist on the chin. He did manage to roll with the blow a little bit, and that was all that kept him from getting knocked back or his jaw broken altogether. When he twisted back around to look into the doorway, Clint was ready for anything.

The man's lips were curled in a vicious smile. Like an animal that had smelled blood, he couldn't help following up his punch with another one hot on its heels. This time, he sent his other hand toward Clint's jaw, determined to knock the sense out of Clint's skull . . .

DON'T MISS THESE
ALL-ACTION WESTERN SERIES
FROM THE BERKLEY PUBLISHING GROUP

THE GUNSMITH by J. R. Roberts
Clint Adams was a legend among lawmen, outlaws, and ladies. They called him . . . the Gunsmith.

LONGARM by Tabor Evans
The popular long-running series about Deputy U.S. Marshal Long—his life, his loves, his fight for justice.

SLOCUM by Jake Logan
Today's longest-running action Western. John Slocum rides a deadly trail of hot blood and cold steel.

BUSHWACKERS by B. J. Lanagan
An action-packed series by the creators of Longarm! The rousing adventures of the most brutal gang of cutthroats ever assembled—Quantrill's Raiders.

DIAMONDBACK by Guy Brewer
Dex Yancey is Diamondback, a Southern gentleman turned con man when his brother cheats him out of the family fortune. Ladies love him. Gamblers hate him. But nobody pulls one over on Dex . . .

WILDGUN by Jack Hanson
The blazing adventures of mountain man Will Barlow—from the creators of Longarm!

TEXAS TRACKER by Tom Calhoun
Meet J.T. Law: the most relentless—and dangerous—manhunter in all Texas. Where sheriffs and posses fail, he's the best man to bring in the most vicious outlaws—for a price.

THE GUNSMITH

277

ROLLING THUNDER

J. R. ROBERTS

JOVE BOOKS, NEW YORK

THE BERKLEY PUBLISHING GROUP
Published by the Penguin Group
Penguin Group (USA) Inc.
375 Hudson Street, New York, New York 10014, USA
Penguin Group (Canada), 10 Alcorn Avenue, Toronto, Ontario M4V 3B2, Canada
(a division of Pearson Penguin Canada Inc.)
Penguin Books Ltd., 80 Strand, London WC2R 0RL, England
Penguin Group Ireland, 25 St. Stephen's Green, Dublin 2, Ireland (a division of Penguin Books Ltd.)
Penguin Group (Australia), 250 Camberwell Road, Camberwell, Victoria 3124, Australia
(a division of Pearson Australia Group Pty. Ltd.)
Penguin Books India Pvt. Ltd., 11 Community Centre, Panchsheel Park, New Delhi—110 017, India
Penguin Group (NZ), Cnr. Airborne and Rosedale Roads, Albany, Auckland 1310, New Zealand
(a division of Pearson New Zealand Ltd.)
Penguin Books (South Africa) (Pty.) Ltd., 24 Sturdee Avenue, Rosebank, Johannesburg 2196, South
Africa

Penguin Books Ltd., Registered Offices: 80 Strand, London WC2R 0RL, England

This is a work of fiction. Names, characters, places, and incidents either are the product of the author's imagination or are used fictitiously, and any resemblance to actual persons, living or dead, business establishments, events, or locales is entirely coincidental.

ROLLING THUNDER

A Jove Book / published by arrangement with the author

PRINTING HISTORY
Jove edition / January 2005

ISBN: 0-515-13878-9

JOVE®
Jove Books are published by The Berkley Publishing Group,
a division of Penguin Group (USA) Inc.
375 Hudson Street, New York, New York 10014.
JOVE is a registered trademark of Penguin Group (USA) Inc.
The "J" design is a trademark belonging to Penguin Group (USA) Inc.

PRINTED IN THE UNITED STATES OF AMERICA

10 9 8 7 6 5 4 3 2 1

ONE

Spring was coming.

Although winter was still in the air, it was losing its grip and the cold was beginning to be swept away by a more favorable wind. There was still plenty of chill to be had, however, as well as plenty of snow on the ground. But those things seemed to have been around for so long that they'd become just another couple of components of the landscape.

Whatever snow that was left was dirty and melting into the grass. The cold breeze was becoming more cool and comforting. All in all, it was a nice time of year. It was the time that made a man feel glad he'd made it through the harder times when he'd been freezing his tail off and fighting to catch his next breath before his lungs were frozen shut.

Those wintery trials weren't too far behind, but they were over and that was all that mattered. Standing on the rickety platform built in what appeared to be the middle of nowhere, the group of people soaked up the wide expanse of scenery and drank in the pleasant weather. There were five people in all, and they stood on that platform waiting for the arrival of the stagecoach that would take them to the closest railroad station.

Every so often, they could hear the sound of an engine rumbling over the tracks. The clatter of wheels on rails wasn't that far away. Of course, the only thing that kept them from walking toward that sound was that the trains didn't make it a habit to stop unless there was a station in sight. Unfortunately, there was no such structure anywhere to be seen, and that left those five people right where they started.

Waiting for that stage.

Waiting to get to their train.

Just waiting.

Having exhausted all their bits of conversation a while back, the people on the platform rocked on their heels and took turns sitting on the little bench made out of weathered planks. They all faced forward with their hands either folded neatly or shoved into pockets. Every so often, one of the people waiting there would get the urge to break the silence.

That didn't usually go over too well.

"Lovely day, isn't it?" an elderly woman wrapped in a bright yellow shawl said to anyone who was listening.

It took a moment for the reply to come and when it did, it seemed to be given only to end the wait for it.

"Yeah," a tall man standing at the front of the platform answered. "It sure is."

A little less than a minute passed before the other man on the platform added, "Yep. Sure 'nuff."

There were a few coughs as well as a clearing of the throat, but not much else was said besides that. It was an odd sight, having those folks standing on the only man-made structure for miles in any direction. All around the platform were open fields, trees, a lonely trail, and plenty of light blue sky stretching out overhead.

Even the nearby animals seemed bored, and they made only slightly more noise than the people did as they skittered through the tall grass or every so often cleared their own throats in one way or another.

When the sound of an approaching horse could be heard, it drew everyone's attention. It came from the south and since the platform's bench was facing north, it meant everyone standing on the platform had to turn around to get a look at the incoming horse.

"I wonder who that could be," the old woman said.

The second man was shorter than the first. He had the lanky build and leathery skin of a farmer. His eyes narrowed as he squinted toward the south, genuinely interested in anything that could change his scenery in the slightest.

"Hard to say from here," he said. "Anyone expectin' someone?"

The others on the platform glanced around and shook their heads before turning their attention back to the approaching horse. The excitement lasted for another few minutes before the horse came to a stop next to the other two horses tied there. Those other horses were tied to a post a few yards from the edge of the platform. Every single one of those animals looked just as bored as the people who owned the saddles on their backs.

Wheezing as though he'd been the one to run all the way to that platform, the man on the horse swung down and landed with both boots on the ground at the same time. "This where I catch the train to Duskin?"

As always, it was the elderly woman who spoke up first. "Not hardly, but this is where the stage picks you up that brings you to the station."

"When's the stage coming?"

"Should be here anytime now."

The new arrival caught his breath and glanced a few times in every direction. Finally, he climbed onto the platform and joined the others. He nodded to everyone standing there and, in no time at all, he seemed to settle into the boredom that gripped every other soul in the vicinity of those weathered boards and that rickety bench.

Less than an hour passed before the new man broke the silence that had become second nature to everyone else. "You said that stage was supposed to be here anytime?"

"That's right," the old woman said with a friendly nod. "Anytime at all."

After looking around at the others on the platform, the new man settled his eyes on a young woman who stood holding the hand of a six-year-old girl. "Will the stage be here soon?"

The young woman had dark brown hair that stopped just short of shoulder length. Her eyes were tired and she shrugged after being asked that question. "It was supposed to be here a while ago. Lord only knows how much longer before it actually shows."

The new man was about to ask the same question of the taller man who stood at the edge of the platform, but stopped when he saw that man look down at him and shake his head. Swallowing the question that still itched at the back of his throat, he let out the breath he'd been holding and fully gave in to his situation.

Like all the others that had arrived before him, the new man picked a spot on the platform for his own and settled into it. From there, he was able to rest his eyes and listen to the sound of the lazy breezes that continued to rustle the nearby grass.

Another hour passed.

The new man was still rooted to his spot with his arms folded across his chest, his eyes closed, and his head sagging down onto his chest. Another set of hooves broke the silence, only this time nobody was inclined to look toward the south to see who was coming.

The horses drew closer, and soon it was obvious that they didn't mean to stop at the platform. When the rumble got closer, a few of the people turned to look. The tall man was one of those, and what he saw seemed to catch and hold his interest.

"Looks like one hell of an animal," the shorter man said after stepping away from the new man to keep from waking him. "Too bad we can't hitch a ride with him instead of waiting for this damn stage."

"Yeah. I'd say those horses aren't going to be stopping for anything anytime soon, though."

"Horses?" After squinting toward the approaching shapes, the shorter man nodded and said, "I'll be damned. You're right about that. There's two of 'em."

The horses were closing in fast. One of them peeled away from the trail while the other picked up speed and thundered toward the left side of the platform.

"Are more friends joining our little gathering?" the old woman asked.

"Someone's coming," the tall man said as he shifted his coat open to reveal the modified Colt strapped to his hip, "but I don't think they're friendly."

TWO

Clint had been standing at that platform, counting the blades of grass in the nearby field, for what seemed like a lifetime. The hours had gone by without much more than scant conversation to fill them. With his own horse, Eclipse, waiting for him in Duskin, he'd felt as though he'd been stranded in the middle of Wyoming.

There was an ancient Chinese proverb that told a man to be careful of what he wished for because he just might get it. Actually, Clint wasn't certain that saying was Chinese in origin, but he did know that he was sure as hell going to get the excitement he'd been craving.

The horse that had broken off from the one that was coming was nowhere to be seen. It had bolted into some nearby trees and was moving too fast to be spotted through the rows of gnarled trunks. That left that first horse, and it was still running straight for the platform.

So far, none of the others seemed too concerned about the rider charging in their direction. There had been a few others and it was, after all, a trail open for anyone to ride. What had caught Clint's attention was the sense of urgency in the horse's pace. Urgency like that could only be caused by a rider putting the spurs to his mount. Beyond that, there was something about the frantic pace that stuck in Clint's craw.

Once the clouds overhead shifted to redirect the sunlight onto the rider properly, Clint spotted the glint of bared steel that confirmed his suspicion. The rider's gun was drawn. Of course, the only problem was that the horse was coming in so fast that it was about to charge straight over them before Clint had time to react.

The horse was moving so slow it was like the trail was coated in lava. As it got closer, the sound of its heavy breathing filled the air. The man in the saddle pulled hard on the reins, shifting the animal's course so that it would come close to the platform without actually stomping over the boards.

There was no time for Clint to call out a warning. Not wanting to cause panic that might very well send people into the path of the charging horse, he launched himself into motion instead.

Everyone else on the platform was rooted to their spots, either out of shock or because they didn't know any better.

The approaching horse bolted toward the group, closing the distance to less than five yards in the blink of an eye. Even Clint was amazed at how quickly the horse was moving. It was because of that amazing speed that he wasn't able to react any quicker.

As it was, he thought he might already be too late.

Clint held off until the last possible moment just in case he was jumping to conclusions about the rider's intentions. As it was, the only way Clint had to jump was away from the edge of the platform since that was where the horse swerved as he got closer.

The rider had been holding his pistol low right up to the last moment. Once he got to within spitting distance of the platform, he raised the weapon and took quick aim. That was all Clint needed to see for him to do the same with his Colt and squeeze off a shot.

No matter how close the horse might have been, it took

on a quick burst of speed that launched it forward faster
than Clint had anticipated. The Colt barked once and sent
its round through the air a foot or two behind its target.

Crouched low over the front of the saddle, the rider was
clinging to the horse's back like he'd been grown there. He
didn't seem rattled in the least by the gunfire, and waited
before pulling his own trigger until he was good and ready.

The second gunshot cracked through the air just as the
new man was looking around and trying to get his bearings
after having been jerked out of his stand-up nap. His eyes
quickly found the source of the disturbance and less than
half a second later, the rider's bullet caught him square between the eyes.

Clint watched the new man's head bust open like a
cracked melon as he started running for the other side of the
platform. Clint pointed the Colt toward the speeding horse,
but was amazed to see that the animal was still picking up
speed. The fraction of a second he lost in readjusting his aim
yet again was enough to buy the rider several more yards.

Clint took another shot, but it was rushed and he knew
only too well that he was going to miss. Before he could
take more careful aim, he saw the horse that had split up
from the other burst into view as it charged for the platform
from the southwest.

Spotting the shotgun that was already butting against
the second rider's shoulder, Clint shifted his aim and fired
a shot. The second horse may have been fast, but it didn't
have the element of surprise and Clint was already poised
to throw more lead into the air.

Clint's bullet plowed through the shotgunner's chest,
plucking him completely off the back of his horse. Spin-
ning back around to where the first rider had headed, he
cursed under his breath and lowered the Colt.

All that remained of that killer's horse was the trembling grass in its wake and the distant sound of rolling
thunder that was its hooves pounding against the dirt.

THREE

The horse was an Appaloosa. Even though the animal itself was just a memory, that memory was fresh enough in Clint's mind to stick there for a good, long while. The bitter stink of burnt gunpowder still hung in the air and the folks on the platform were shifting around nervously as if they didn't know where to go or what to do with themselves.

Those people were frightened for a good reason. After all, a gunman had just ridden by and blasted one of the people among them straight to hell. Also, not too far from the platform, the horse that had made the second charge was still standing by the body of its rider, which was twisted in a tangle of limbs in the spot where Clint had dropped him.

For a few moments, however, Clint stood there silently watching the spot where that Appaloosa had charged away through the trees to the north of the platform. Those few moments ticked away slowly, but when they were over, Clint found himself in the middle of a chaotic mess.

"Who were those men?"

"Where did they come from?"

"Oh, my God! I think they're coming back for us!"

"Why'd they kill that man?"

"Are you sure? Are they coming back?"

There were plenty more questions filling the air, but those were only a few of the ones that Clint could actually understand amid the constant flow of frightened chatter. Holstering his Colt and turning toward the people on the platform, Clint threw himself into the mess and did the best he could to keep it from getting any worse.

"Everybody just calm down!" Clint shouted so he could be heard above everyone else.

Perhaps it was the tone of his voice that caught everyone's attention, but it seemed more likely that they all stopped because he was the only one still there who'd drawn iron and fired off a shot. Whatever the reason, Clint wasn't about to split hairs.

Now that the chatter had stopped and everyone was looking at him, Clint lowered his voice and held out his open hands to show there were no more guns to worry about. "We need to keep our heads here, everyone. Getting all panicked won't do anyone any good."

"Keep our heads?" the shorter man asked. "Keep our heads!? There's two dead men here and for all we know, that maniac will circle around to—"

"Stop right there," Clint said, wanting to nip another wave of panic in the bud. "Just be quiet and listen."

They did as they were told, although their eyes were all darting around at any and every trace of movement.

The brunette with the shoulder-length hair kept her eyes fixed on Clint once she'd calmed down the little girl clinging to her arm. "What are we listening for?" she asked. "I don't hear anything."

Clint nodded once. "Exactly. If that rider was coming back, we'd hear the horse just like we did the first time. Until we hear him coming back, we can assume he's gone."

The truth of the matter was that Clint didn't put much faith in not being able to hear those hooves beating against the ground. The gunman could be circling around on foot or in any number of quieter ways, but Clint figured he'd keep alert for that. It was more important for the others to calm down.

Clint's explanation seemed to have the desired effect. At least, it did to some degree. The people were breathing a little easier and didn't seem so ready to scatter away from that platform in five different directions.

"All right then," Clint said. "I want everyone to make sure they're okay and didn't catch any stray bullets. I'm going over there to move that body."

As soon as Clint stepped off the platform, he felt the fear from the others fill the air like the prickle of a nearby lightning strike. "It's all right," he said assuringly. "I won't go far."

Clint headed over to where the body was lying, and got a little hassle from the dead man's horse as he approached it. The animal snorted and bobbed its head, but that's about all the fussing it put up before allowing Clint to kneel down and get closer to the corpse.

It wasn't a pleasant task, but there were questions to be answered and the only one nearby who could do that was the man lying on the ground in a heap. Clint patted the body down quickly, but it didn't take long to realize that there wasn't much on the body that would be of any help. The dead man's pockets were empty; apart from extra rounds for his weapon, the dead man didn't have much to offer.

Clint took hold of the body under the arms and dragged it into the bushes and out of sight. From there, he approached the horse and reached out to calm the animal by stroking its mane and talking quietly to it to calm its jangled nerves.

"Easy there," Clint whispered. "I'm not going to hurt you."

The horse may not have understood the words, but the intention was clear enough and eventually the animal let

Clint approach unopposed. There wasn't much to see on the horse either. The saddlebags weren't even half full, and most of that was a few supplies and some sticks of beef jerky.

"What're you doing?" the shorter man asked from where he was perched on the edge of the platform.

Without looking back, Clint kept digging in the saddlebags and replied, "Just having a look at what this fellow might have been carrying."

"What're you looking for? Whatever money you find isn't—"

"He's probably looking for something besides money," the brunette cut in, using an aggravated tone. "After what he did for us, I'd think you'd be more willing to give him more credit than that."

"Thank you," Clint said to her as his hand touched upon something that he'd almost missed altogether.

Her eyes turned to him and she asked, "You are looking for something besides money, right?"

Clint removed what he'd found, which was a folded-up piece of paper. "I sure am. In fact, I might have just found something that'll help us a whole lot better than his pocket change."

FOUR

Clint returned to the platform and stood up there with everyone else. Although there was plenty of space around the little structure, nobody wanted to leave it. They stayed on those planks like they were on a raft in the middle of an ocean and to step off would be to drown. Rather than argue with that logic, Clint went along with it. At least everyone was staying together.

Someone had used what appeared to be a knit blanket to cover the body of the man who'd been shot dead by the rider. When he looked around, Clint saw the old woman was missing her shawl. The gray-haired woman was holding up pretty well under the circumstances, and had found comfort in tending to the little girl accompanied by the brunette.

With the little girl in good hands for the moment, the brunette walked up to where Clint was standing and said, "Thank you, mister."

Clint looked up from the paper he'd found and caught himself staring into the rich, alluring mixture of gold and brown in her eyes. "No need to thank me. They were charging all of us."

She reached out and put her hand on his arm. Keeping

her eyes focused on him, she said, "But you were the one who stepped up and put a stop to them, even though you're not the only one wearing a gun."

From the corner of his eye, Clint noticed how the shorter man cringed when he overheard her say that. Even though Clint had noticed that man was heeled, he didn't expect him to draw down on some rampaging killer. Then again, the brunette did have a good point.

"What did you find there?" the brunette asked, now that she knew her point had been made.

"It's a schedule for the stage we're meeting," Clint said, holding the paper out so she could see.

When she leaned in to get a better look, Clint couldn't help but notice the smooth contour of her neck as well as the soft, inviting texture of her skin.

"This stop and day are circled," she pointed out. "And so are that stop and day before it."

"Yeah, two days before it to be exact."

"What do you think that means?"

"I'm not certain, but it's the only thing we've got that points in any direction at all. Do you know who that man is?" Clint asked, nodding down at the body covered in the old woman's shawl.

The brunette shrugged. "The first time I saw him was when he came riding up here. Actually, I don't even know who you are."

Clint smiled and held out his free hand. "I'm Clint Adams. I guess it's been rude of me to keep to myself all these hours we've been standing here."

"Don't feel bad. You're not the only one that's been quiet up until now. My name's Krista. Krista Myers."

Her hand was warm and soft in Clint's grasp. When he shook it, he also felt a strength in her grip that matched up with the easy confidence in her voice. With her remaining so close to him, he could start to pick up on her scent, which had a hint of a spicy, yet subtle perfume.

"Clint Adams," she repeated. "Have I heard that name before?"

"Clint Adams?" the short man said, his head snapping up like a dog who'd just caught whiff of a steak. "You're Clint Adams?"

"Yes, I am."

"The Gunsmith?"

Clint shrugged in a way that acknowledged the title without fully encouraging it.

"That explains that fancy shooting. Bill Grady. Pleased to meet you!"

As Bill stepped forward and shook Clint's hand, the old woman did the same. She introduced herself simply as Martha, and sat back down again after offering her quick thanks.

Before Clint could turn back to Krista, he stopped before knocking over the one last person on the platform he had yet to meet. The little girl stood solidly in front of Clint, and straightened her posture even more once she saw that he was looking straight down at her.

"My name is Catherine," she said proudly. "But my friends call me Cat."

Clint squatted down to her level and held out his hand. "I've met a few other Catherines in my day," he said. "But not one as pretty as you."

The girl blushed and fidgeted on her feet. There was still some worry in her eyes, and she did her best to keep from looking at the figure shrouded under the shawl. Even so, the girl managed to force the smile back onto her face.

"You can call me Cat."

"All right then, Cat. Can you do me a favor?"

She nodded.

Moving just a little closer, Clint dropped his voice to a stage whisper and said, "Try to keep everyone from getting too upset. We shouldn't have to wait here too much longer."

Having that little task to do was enough to put some more wind in Cat's sails and she spun back around to get to work.

Bill was right there to fill Clint's field of vision once he straightened back up again.

"Wait here?" the shorter man asked. "The hell I am! After what happened?"

"Look here," Clint said. "The last thing we need to do is split up. Once that stage comes, that means there'll be more people with us and there's always more safety in numbers."

"Yeah, but I'd rather—"

Bill was cut off by the rumble of approaching horses. Everyone heard that and froze like deer caught in a hunter's sights. Clint's hand hovered over the Colt's grip as he moved to stand at the edge of the platform facing toward the source of the noise.

The rumble got louder with every passing second, and once the horses came into view, the stagecoach they were pulling immediately followed. Every one of them let out a sigh of relief and quickly gathered their things.

Pulling up to the platform, the stagecoach driver looked down at the mess and asked, "What the hell happened here?"

"Let's just get out of here," Clint said while helping Martha, Cat, and Krista into the stage. "I'll explain along the way."

FIVE

Clint only had to explain things to the driver of the stage for about ten seconds before he was given a job for the ride into Duskin. Even though they had a man to ride shotgun, dealing with a killer who'd already attacked their passengers wasn't exactly what that man had signed on for.

"I'll hold my post," the shotgunner told Clint, "but I'm not going to be much good against someone who did the likes of that."

When he said that, the shotgunner nodded toward the bodies laying on the ground near the stage.

"What my friend here is trying to say, Mr. Adams," the driver explained, "is that you're a hell of a lot better shot than he is with any kind of iron. I wouldn't presume to give you orders, but—"

"Say no more," Clint interrupted. "I'd prefer to keep an eye out for any more trouble anyhow. But I will need some help in loading those bodies onto those horses."

Bill looked over to the pair of horses being tethered onto the back of the stage so they could be taken along for the ride. His eyes got wider as he saw Clint and the two men running the stage walk over toward the animals.

"Now hold on here," Bill said. "My horse ain't up to this

long of a ride carrying a load like that. If he was, I
wouldn't have needed to book passage on this wagon!"

Martha was the one to answer him first. "We've all got
to do our part here, Bill." Looking to Clint, she added, "My
horse can carry both of those men into town."

"Are you sure about that?" Clint asked.

"Of course. She's strong enough. The only one not up to
the ride into Duskin is me. I just borrowed that horse from
my son to get me to where I needed to meet up with this
stage. Now that I'm here, you can put the horse to work."

"All right then. At least some folks are willing to chip in."

Waiting until the first body was strapped onto the back
of Martha's horse, Bill finally gave in and let out an exasperated sigh. "Fine. Put the other on my horse. But if it gets
hurt dragging that carcass along the way, I expect to be re-
imbursed for my loss."

"Just forget it, Bill," Clint said. "That other fellow's
horse is still here, so we'll tie him to that one instead."

"But, I don't mind if you—"

"Just save it. God forbid you do anything of any value
along the way."

Clint's tone was harsh and he'd spoken those words
without thinking about it first. Even though he didn't mean
to cut the man off at the knees like that, he was too damn
tired to take it back. At this point in the day, none of the
other men were too anxious to deal with Bill's whining either. Clint was at the top of this list since his patience
tended to wear thin once he found himself under fire for no
apparent reason.

For better or worse, the matter was settled. After that, it
didn't take long before everybody was loaded onto whatever was taking them and the entire group was on its way.

The stagecoach moved along at a healthy pace, even
considering the extra burden being hauled by the two
horses tethered to its back. With only two other passengers
apart from the ones that had been waiting at the platform,

the stage got up to a steady pace. Bill rode with the women and children while Clint rode up front with the driver. The stage's regular shotgunner sat at the back of the coach with his legs dangling over the side. From there, he could keep an eye out for any unwanted company.

The only faces the shotgunner saw for the rest of the trip were those of the horses carrying the bodies wrapped in their jackets. Since they were only carrying the loads on their backs, those horses didn't have any trouble keeping up with the stagecoach's pace. In fact, they seemed to enjoy the leisurely ride much more than the people on or in the coach itself.

Once they were on their way and that damn platform was far behind him, Clint started to enjoy the ride a bit himself. The air was crisp and clean, carrying that special scent that only came in the days when the seasons were shifting around him. Winter was on its way out and spring wasn't far away, so that left them with a good taste of both times.

With nobody else in sight throughout the entire trip, it seemed as though they had the whole trail to themselves. The stagecoach rumbled along its route, keeping its wheels firmly inside the twin ruts that marked the way to Duskin.

"How's it going back there?" Clint asked.

Behind him, the stage's regular shotgunner gave a quick wave and replied, "Can't see nothing but the dust we're kicking up."

"Sounds good to me."

So far, the driver had been fairly quiet. Clint had filled him in on what had happened with the attack on the platform, but that only caused the driver to keep more to himself. Now that he'd had some time to digest what had happened, he glanced somewhat nervously over to Clint.

"Uhh . . . you don't think that man that rode off will be coming back, do you?"

"Not right away," Clint answered. "Maybe not at all. I'd

like to say more for sure, but I don't even know who those men are. There's a lawman in Duskin who might be able to give me a name or two."

"You mean Marshal Wise?"

"Yeah. You know Sam?"

"I've met him on occasion. But then again, I try to keep those occasions down to a minimum."

Clint smiled at the comment and added, "Me too actually. Sam's a good fellow, but he's been dealing with some unsavory sorts lately."

"Is that why you're headed into Duskin?"

"Pretty much. I was in the area and thought I'd drop in for a visit. When I got there, I saw Sam was short a few deputies and figured I could lend him a hand."

The driver nodded and snapped his reins. His team was small, but it was moving the stage along at a pace that got brisker with every flick of leather across their backs. Of course, that added speed probably had something to do with the growing nervousness of the man urging them on.

"So," the driver said, "you're planning to hire on as a lawman for a spell?"

Clint shook his head. "Not exact—" He cut his reply short when his eyes fixed upon something moving across the horizon not too far to the right. The driver picked up on his alertness and started darting his eyes back and forth.

"You see something, Mr. Adams?"

But Clint quickly let out the breath he held and shook his head. "Nah. Thought I did for a moment there, but it's nothing. Anyway, I meant to say that I'm not taking the job of a lawman as such, but I am running a few of Sam's errands. One of them had me escorting a wagon hauling a payroll down into Denver. That's how I wound up standing on the wrong platform at the wrong time."

"Wrong time? We were right on sched—" This time, the driver cut himself off before chuckling nervously and shooting a backward glance toward the gruesome load being carried by the other horses. "Oh, yeah. I see what you mean."

Clint nodded and returned the driver's smile. It didn't take an expert in human nature to notice the tension in the driver's face or the way he kept clearing his throat and shifting in his seat.

Another flick of the reins and the team was going even faster.

SIX

Duskin was a good-sized cow town situated about a day's ride from Fort Laramie. Although it had started out as a place that only stayed up to keep the cowboys in food and drink, Duskin had taken on a life of its own, and had even prospered some along the way. It was quiet enough to raise a family, yet active enough for the local marshal to feel the strain after losing the brothers who had acted as his deputies for the last few years.

Clint had been there a few times, and recognized the sight of it the moment the first several buildings came into view. The ride should have taken the better part of two days, but everyone agreed that they were in no mood to camp and would hunker down for a faster ride no matter how rough it might be.

With the horses pulling the stage at full speed on and off, everyone inside and on top of the stage was jostled to the point that their teeth were rattling. By the time they got close enough to Duskin to see the shape of the town in the distance, everyone let out a tired, yet heartfelt, cheer.

Pulling into the town at a time that was too late to be evening and too early to be morning, the stage was greeted by a sleepy-eyed and confused old man wearing a jacket and britches pulled on hastily over a set of long underwear. The old man carried a lantern in one hand and kept sneaking glances to the eastern sky.

"It ain't morning yet, is it?" he asked in a scratchy voice.

Clint dropped down from the stage and approached the familiar old man. "Not yet, Gus, but it's getting close to that time."

Squinting through sagging eyelids and holding the lantern up a bit higher, the old man asked, "That you, Clint?"

"Sure is, old-timer. Looks like your eyes aren't as bad as you thought."

"There ain't nothin' wrong with my eyes. They're just tired and surprised to see you so early. I wasn't expectin' to see you till tomorrow."

Clint walked around to the side of the coach and opened the door. "We're running a little ahead of schedule. Nobody much seemed to mind, though."

Gus looked over to the other two men on the stage. The driver hopped down and didn't even bother taking a breath before getting right back to work. The shotgunner was already pulling the baggage down from the top of the stage and was handing it to the driver's waiting arms.

"What's the hurry there?" Gus asked the driver, who stood nearby. "I'm sure those things'll be fine up there if you want to stretch your legs for a bit."

"There'll be time for that later," the driver said. "I'll relax once this is done and I get some whiskey in me."

Narrowing his eyes as though he was seeing something he didn't much like, Gus turned to Clint, who was helping the passengers out of the stage. "There's something you need to tell me, Adams."

Clint didn't answer right away, since he was busy helping Martha down to the street.

Gus stood aside as passengers started walking past him.

He noticed the troubled look in their eyes, and then spotted the two heavy shapes draped over the backs of two of the spare horses. "You definitely got something to say to me, Clint. There's always more goin' on when you're part of this much nervousness. If it was anyone else, I'd say you were all just tuckered out, but I know better."

"Is Sam around?" Clint asked.

"Aw, Jesus. Already asking for the marshal? What the hell went on out there? Did that payroll make it through?"

"Since you already know everything going on in this place," Clint said, "maybe Sam should give you the job he's constantly trying to put on my shoulders."

"I wouldn't have none of it. I'm too old for this nonsense."

"Then why start worrying about it now?"

"But isn't that . . . aren't those . . ." Gus got closer to Clint and dropped his voice to a whisper as if any sound could be hidden in the predawn hush enveloping the world. "Aren't those bodies on them horses?"

"Yeah, they are," Clint replied, without even trying to lower his voice. "And I'm too tired to deal with them or much of anything else right now. All of these folks and I have been on this stage for too long without any rest just so we could get here that much quicker. Now that we're here, we aim to get some sleep and that's it. Everything else will still be here in the morning."

"Speak for yourself," the stage's driver said after tossing down the last of the baggage. "I'm getting a few drinks before I do anything else."

"And then?" Clint asked.

Shrugging, the driver answered, "Sleep."

"Close enough. Gus, I'll be in my room at The Carroll House. If something comes up, you know how to get ahold of me." Before walking away from the stage with the other passengers, Clint added, "But I'd think twice about waking me up if I were you."

SEVEN

It was amazing what a few hours of sleep could do for a man. The sun wasn't too high in the sky when Clint rolled over in his rented bed and pulled his eyelids apart. Daylight poured through his window, bathing him in warmth that added to the comfort provided by his soft blankets and fresh linens.

Normally, Clint followed his instincts and woke up as soon as his eyes came open on their own. This time, however, he closed them again and pulled in a deep breath. The only way to describe that breath was that it smelled like morning. It was filled with so many different scents that it just blended together to remind him more of a general time rather than anything too specific.

He could smell breakfast being cooked, fresh air drifting through his window, as well as the smoky remnants of fires being put out or stoked in homes and businesses all up and down the street. The sunlight warming the wood of the walls and floors even gave off a kind of smell. That scent was probably something else entirely, but Clint enjoyed the sensations too much to look at them too closely. Instead, he'd decided long ago to just savor them the way he did any other of life's simple pleasures.

Someone was walking heavily up and down the hall. Clint could hear the clatter of heels knocking against the floorboards, and decided that it was time to get himself up after all. As nice as it would have been to sleep the day away, there were still matters that needed to be settled and people waiting to have him explain the two new bodies that had been ridden into town the night before.

Clint got out of bed and took his time in getting dressed. When he was pulling on his boots, he noticed the sound that had caught his attention a couple minutes ago. It was that same patter of heels against wood, only this time he could tell that they weren't going back and forth outside his door the way he'd previously thought.

The staccato tapping was coming from outside, but it was staying in one place. That one place just happened to be in the hall directly outside his room. Every so often, the tapping would stop. Before long, however, it would start all over again. It wouldn't be any harder or faster, but just another chorus of something knocking against wood like urgent feet hustling along their way.

When Clint got up, he reflexively reached for his gun belt and strapped it around his waist. The weight of the modified Colt felt just as familiar to him as the shirt on his back or the hat upon his head. Sometimes, he didn't even realize the gun was there at all. One thing was for certain, however. He would have known the instant it wasn't.

Those weren't footsteps. Clint knew that now that he was listening intently and not distracted with other things. Reaching out, he pulled the door open to find a small, fresh face staring right back up at him.

"Good morning, Mr. Adams," Cat said. The little girl sounded like she was reciting the greeting for her teacher, and made Clint feel about twenty years older.

"Morning, Cat."

"Didn't you hear me knocking?"

"I sure did, but . . . well, I guess I'm still a little tired."

"Aunt Krista says that not getting enough sleep can make your eyes get baggy."

Clint smiled and knelt down so he was at her eye level. "Well, take a look for yourself."

The little girl scrunched up her face and took a good, long look. She took so much time doing so, in fact, that Clint was starting to wonder if she'd really found something to worry about. Finally, she stepped back, shrugged, and said, "They're just little ones. You probably only need a nap later."

"That sounds pretty good." Looking into the hallway, Clint asked, "Did you come here all by yourself?"

"No."

"All right then. Who did you come here with?"

"Aunt Krista."

"Is she waiting for us?"

Suddenly, Cat's eyes widened and she burst into motion so quickly that it seemed someone had lit a fire under her. "She's waiting downstairs! Come on," she insisted, taking hold of Clint by the hand and pulling him along. "Come with me. We're going to have breakfast!"

Clint allowed himself to be tugged out of his room, and shut the door behind him. Once she saw that she'd accomplished her mission, Cat slowed down just enough to keep from tossing Clint down the stairs.

"I used to live here," Cat explained.

"In this hotel?"

"No, silly! In this town."

"Oh. My next guess was going to be that you lived in the stable with the hay and horses."

Cat looked up at him as though Clint had just started barking like a dog. When she saw him smile and give her a little wink, she broke out into a fit of giggles that lasted all the way down the stairs to where Krista was waiting.

"He's funny," Cat said, clenching Clint's hand even tighter.

Krista couldn't help but laugh a bit as well. The girl's giggling was so cheery that it was infectious. "She didn't interrupt anything did she, Clint?"

"No, not at all."

"Did she wake you up? I told her not to wake you up if she thought you were sleeping."

"I didn't wake him up!" Cat said in her own defense. After thinking about that for a moment, she looked up at Clint and asked, "I didn't, did I?"

"Almost, but not quite. Tell you what, though. Show me where I can get some breakfast and we'll call it even."

Cat smiled again and started marching to the room that was practically busting with people. "Right this way."

Once Cat was a few paces ahead of them, Krista looked over to Clint and said, "I hope it's all right that we came to fetch you this morning. I just thought it'd be nice if—"

"No need to explain," Clint said. "This is nice. After the way I spent yesterday, this is just a few steps shy of heaven."

"Heaven may be pushing it a bit," Krista said. "Let's just start off with some pancakes."

EIGHT

Breakfast couldn't have been better. After the monotony of waiting at the platform the other day followed by the excitement of getting put into the line of fire, sitting at a table across from Cat and Krista over a stack of flapjacks was a blessing. They talked about a lot of nothing and by the time they were through, Clint wasn't even thinking about anything more than his full stomach.

Of course, that kind of contentment rarely lasted long.

"I suppose you're going to see Marshal Wise soon," Krista said.

Clint nodded. "Yeah, I suppose I should."

"You were working for him, weren't you?"

"For the time being."

"I've seen you around town here and there. Actually, I just spotted you once or twice before I went to pick up Cat."

The little girl nudged her aunt with a little bony elbow. "You said he was a tall, hands—"

"That'll be enough of that, young lady," Krista said in a stern voice.

But Cat knew better than to take the scolding too seriously. Instead, she pursed her mouth shut and sat ponder-

29

ing how much more she could get away with saying. She thought better of it when she saw the look on Krista's face.

"Anyway," Krista said, "we've all heard about someone like you taking up the slack for Marshal Wise, but I never thought it was really The Gunsmith himself."

Rolling his eyes at the sound of that nickname, Clint said, "That was my idea. Sometimes if the wrong people find out a man like me is working for the law in a town, those people take it upon themselves to drop down on that town like a pack of hungry dogs."

"Then again, you must be used to folks finding out who you are."

"Yeah, I am. It's nice to go unnoticed sometimes, though."

Krista smiled and nodded.

Listening intently to everything that had been said, Cat was unable to contain herself any longer. "I think my aunt noticed you a long time ago."

This time, Krista was too surprised by what had come out of her niece's mouth to react before the words were already said. One look at the child caused Cat to clamp her mouth shut and hunker down over what was left of her breakfast.

"Sorry about that, Clint," Krista said. "Every so often, Cat doesn't know when to quit."

"It seems like she knows what she's talking about," Clint said, pausing just long enough for Krista's cheeks to start to blush. "You both notice a lot that goes on around here. Is there any chance that you've ever seen the man that was shot before?"

Obviously, Krista wasn't expecting the conversation to turn like that. She seemed relieved that it did, but she was still surprised nonetheless. "Umm, actually I may have seen him, but that would have been it. I surely don't know his name or why anyone would want to gun him down. Do you think those killers thought he was someone else?"

"I doubt that." Clint was about to say more, but he noticed that Cat was still listening intently to the conversation. Rather than dredge up any more bad memories or get into any gruesome details, Clint simply said, "It's over, though. That's all that matters."

Krista saw the way Clint glanced over to the little girl, and understood why he was cutting the topic short. "That's right, Clint," she said, patting the little girl's hand. "Those men are gone and they won't be coming back."

Clint smiled, nodded, and used the remains of his last biscuit to sop up what was left of his melted butter and syrup. He could see that Cat was getting bored and anxious to leave, which was a whole lot better than being frightened at the talk of death and bad men.

More than anything, Clint wanted to sweep the topic under the table and forget about it altogether. Unfortunately, things didn't work that way. Bad men had a nasty habit of doing bad things, and death only too often surrounded them.

"Are you staying with us, Mr. Adams?" Cat asked, snapping him out of his darkening thoughts.

Clint forced a smile onto his face that didn't even seem to fool the little girl. "I'm not going anywhere for a while, but I do have some things to tend to."

With that, the adults stood up from the table and were quickly joined by Cat. Krista took her hand and started walking toward the hotel's front door. Once outside, all three of them stopped under the shade of the building's front awning.

"Please keep me up on what's going on, Clint," Krista asked. "About everything, that is."

"Sure thing. I hope this won't be the last time I see you ladies."

Krista smiled and looked more than a little relieved. "It doesn't have to be. Why don't I let you take care of what you need to do for now and you can find me whenever you like."

"That sounds good."

Clint listened as Krista told him where she stayed in town, and then they parted ways. It was a pleasant enough way to spend the morning, but as the time wore on, the shadow of what had happened before kept looming larger and larger in the back of Clint's mind.

He knew only too well that the man killed on that platform wasn't just something that was going to dry up and blow away if he sidestepped the topic long enough. That stagecoach's last stop was in Duskin, which meant that the dead man had intended to come to that town as well. It followed reasonably enough that whatever business he was wrapped in had roots in Duskin as well.

Clint had no idea what that business may have been, but it was enough to get at least one man killed.

He'd put off talking to the marshal long enough. It was time to roll up his sleeves and get back to work. Clint had a fair amount of confidence in Marshal Wise, but the lawman was already shorthanded. It looked like Clint's earlier words had been only too accurate. He wasn't about to leave town anytime soon.

NINE

Zack Michaels was an even-tempered sort of fellow who never seemed to get too riled up about much of anything. He was a good man who provided not only for his family, but for any others who might be in need. That was the way all of his neighbors saw him and he'd never done anything to prove them wrong.

He had a face that looked younger than his forty-eight years simply because it always wore the same easygoing expression. Over the last few weeks, that had changed quite a bit. Zack seemed to be carrying a weight on his shoulders that made him look a few years older with every passing day.

He looked positively reborn when he turned the corner and got a look at the front of the large, flat building that served as a combination stable and ticketing office for the local stagecoach line. His eyes widened and his steps quickened until he was almost running up to the front door, which was propped open by a battered chair.

"Hey, Gus, when did this stage get here?"

The grizzled old man had been tending to some of the horses in the stable. Those animals still looked worn out from the previous day's ride, and were savoring the fact that they could just stand still for a while. Jumping slightly at the sudden noise, Gus dropped the brush he'd been using to smooth down one of the horse's coats.

"Christ Almighty, you scared me!" Gus rasped.

"Sorry about that. I've just been waiting to hear the stage pull in and was beginning to think something had happened."

"Well, the stage got back last night. It was ahead of schedule, that's for certain, but—"

"Ahead of schedule," Zack interrupted. "That's great. That's just great!"

"Well, now there was some—"

"Where are the passengers?" It was plain to see that Zack wasn't paying attention to more than half of what the older man was saying. There was so much going on inside his own head that Zack could barely contain it all. "Are they at the hotel? Did anyone ask for me?"

"Nobody mentioned much, but they had a lot else to think about after the trip and everything that hap—"

"Of course they didn't ask about me. Nobody needed to ask." Blinking a few times, Zack looked at Gus as though it was the first time he'd truly taken notice of the older man. "Thanks for your help, Gus. I really appreciate it."

"But I didn't—"

"Oh, you sure did, Gus. Thanks again!" And with that, Zack spun around on his heels and charged back outside and down the street.

Gus looked after him with no small amount of confusion on his face. "—didn't get to tell you about the bodies," the old man finished, even though there was nobody but horses there to listen.

After scratching his head, Gus bent down to pick up his brush and get back to work. "You see now," he said to the tired horse who'd been one of the animals pulling the stagecoach, "this is why I prefer to talk to the likes of you. It's a whole lot less aggravating."

• • •

Zack was so relieved he could barely even think straight. All this time, he'd been fretting and worrying about what would happen if the stage never came back. He'd thought through every possible scenario, as well as a few he'd made up that just made him worry even more.

Now that he'd seen that familiar stage again with his own two eyes, Zack felt as though his troubles were just being lifted right off his shoulders. Sure, there were still some things that needed to be sorted out, but if things had gotten as bad as he'd imagined, that stage wouldn't be sitting outside that stable just as pretty as you please.

Rushing down the street without even thinking about the steps he took, Zack felt more and more like his old self. Once again, he was smiling to the folks he passed and returning the waves he got as though he didn't have a care in the world. He headed straight through the business district, and quickened his pace once he saw the large homes built a few streets over.

Those were the homes owned by the same men who owned most of the bigger businesses in town. They were ornate, sprawling affairs that made the more modest homes nearby look positively miniscule in comparison. Although he didn't head toward the largest of the homes, Zack made a straight line for one of the contenders for that title.

Opening the gate of a whitewashed fence, Zack stepped through and trotted up a walkway that was well cared for and bordered with shrubs and flowers that were only a few months away from blooming. The house was two floors high and topped with a single gable that marked an attic not quite big enough to be a third floor. Zack noticed movement coming from behind that uppermost window, which made the smile on his face that much wider.

"Larry! Welcome home," Zack shouted as he approached the front door. "Open up and we can celebrate your triumphant return."

The door was closed, but not locked. Zack discovered

that much when he tested the knob. Easing the door open just enough so he could peek inside, Zack shouted, "Hello in there! You're probably tired, so I'll just let myself in."

There was no answer, but Zack could hear the sounds of someone moving around upstairs. Since he was used to entering the big house and making himself at home, he did just that and walked into the parlor where the cart of wine and liquor was kept.

"I'll just pour us some drinks. Hopefully, we've got a lot to celebrate."

Then there were steps coming down the stairs, and Zack turned around with a fresh glass of red wine. The moment he saw who was coming down the stairs, Zack's smile turned into an expression of gaping terror and the glass slid from his hand.

"Why don't you pour me a drink while you're at it," the other man said. "We do have plenty to talk about."

TEN

The office of Marshal Sam Wise was located at the end of Sixth Street. It was a modest building that had obviously been there longer than half of the structures in the business and saloon districts. Even so, it had a solid look about it that made it seem it would be one of the few buildings left standing after any number of natural disasters rolled through.

Clint walked up to the building and stepped inside to find Marshal Wise standing at the coat rack with his jacket pulled halfway on. The lawman looked at him with a bit of surprise, mixed with a friendly smile.

"Well, Clint, if I didn't know any better I'd say you could read minds. I was just on my way to track you down."

"You would've found me easily enough," Clint replied. "I only just woke up and left my hotel."

"Your ears must've been burning because I've been talking about you for the better part of two days now."

The office wasn't too big, but it seemed large simply because it was so empty. There were four desks in all, only two of which had anything more than dust on top of them. The gun racks were either closed and locked or empty altogether. The few vacant jail cells lined up along the back wall looked like hotel rooms that had been lived in but not straightened up again.

"Doesn't look like you've been too busy while I've been gone, Sam."

The marshal shook his head and finished pulling on his jacket. "There were a few dustups, but nothing I couldn't handle. Things around here have certainly quieted down since you decided to lend a hand. You sure I can't convince you to let me pin a badge on you? I could get you a nice salary."

"We discussed this already."

"I know, I know. You don't look too happy, Clint. What's wrong?"

"There was a problem."

"Does it have anything to do with them bodies you dragged in along with that stage?"

"Nothing gets by you," Clint said.

The marshal walked toward the door and gave Clint a friendly slap on the shoulder as he passed by. "Come on with me as I make my rounds. You can tell me all about what happened. I've been aching to hear the news, but figured you could use your rest before answering a whole lot of questions."

Clint fell into step beside the marshal as he started walking his normal route through town. As with any lawman, a big part of his job was just being seen and keeping an eye on things in general. That involved a lot of footwork when there was just one man wearing a badge in a town the size of Duskin.

Although Clint had been lending the marshal a hand in performing his duties, he'd made it known that his was just a temporary situation. Clint had too much associated with his name to wear a badge. More often than not, any sort of fame that involved a gun only brought more trouble to the man who'd earned that reputation.

There were always punks out there looking to make a

name for themselves, as well as those who just had something to prove to the biggest dog in the yard. All Clint had to do to solidify his opinion was think back to conversations he'd had with a man by the name of Wyatt Earp. Any of the Earps could tell him about the trials that came along with being a well-known lawman.

The difference was that the Earp brothers had the law in their blood, while Clint just liked to help out wherever he could. Of course, sometimes that desire to help got him in just as much trouble as trying to bring peace to a rowdy cow town.

"What's on yer mind?" Marshal Wise asked once they'd turned a corner and fallen into their normal path for patrolling the streets.

Clint laughed and answered, "Just thinking about your offer and why I keep turning it down."

"Now there's something I'd like to hear."

"It started out because I didn't want to bring any trouble to your town. Only thing is that trouble always seems to find its way to me no matter what I do."

"And that brings us back to them bodies."

"It sure does."

Pulling in a deep breath as if bracing himself to be punched in the stomach, Marshal Wise clasped his hands behind his back and said, "All right then. Let's hear it."

Clint then set about telling the lawman about what had happened. He didn't give every last detail, but then again he didn't have to. Marshal Wise was good at his job and could fill in some of the blanks on his own. Every so often, Wise would nod or ask to have something cleared up, but for the most part he simply kept walking and let Clint tell his story.

When he reached the end of the tale, Clint felt as if something was missing. "I don't know why, but I thought there was more to it," he told the marshal. "I didn't leave anything out, but it just seems sort of . . . I don't know . . . light."

"It always does when you just tell the bare facts of things like that. I've had plenty of lead thrown my way and it makes every second seem like your last. Once you take that out of the mix, that just leaves a lot of smoke and noise."

"Yeah, I know that just as well, but there's still something else." After a moment, Clint snapped himself out of his thoughts and said, "Oh, I did get a look in the dead man's pockets. I found this."

Clint handed over the folded paper he'd discovered. Halting in his tracks, the marshal examined the schedule and noticed the same two circled dates. His brow furrowed and he nodded.

"This first date strikes a chord with me, Clint, but I don't want to say for sure until I check on it myself."

"What is it, Sam?"

"It's something I read in a newspaper brought over from Cheyenne. But let me get to work on this and you can go over to the undertaker's and do some checking of your own."

"You want to see if anything came up regarding those bodies?"

"You never know. Maybe someone along the way recognized one of 'em. Anyhow, you go check on that and I'll see what I can find about this schedule."

Right about then, Clint was glad he'd started the day off with such a good breakfast. By the looks of things, it was all going to be downhill from there.

ELEVEN

Although Clint had sent plenty of men to the undertaker in his years, he'd rarely had occasion to visit one himself. Like most other folks, he wasn't exactly chomping at the bit to see the grave digger ply his gruesome trade, and didn't have much curiosity about what needed to be done before someone was put into their box.

Walking into the undertaker's parlor, Clint had at least one good thing to say: It was quiet.

"Hello?" Clint said into the narrow room that looked something like a cross between a chapel and a showroom.

Most of the space was taken up with rows of pews that led up to a platform that would hold the casket of the deceased. Branching off from the side of that room was a smaller area set up to display different items ranging from linens to candles to samples of headstones as well as the caskets themselves.

Clint could hear someone working in a room further inside the building, and so he kept walking through the chapel and toward a narrow door behind the raised platform. Before he could make it all the way to the back of the room, Clint saw that narrow door pop open and a spindly man wearing spectacles poke his head through.

"Did someone say something?" the skinny man asked. His eyes quickly found Clint, which caused him to scurry through the door and wipe his hands on the apron he was wearing.

Clint stepped forward and tried not to think about what might have been on the smaller fellow's hands. "Hello there. I'm here on behalf of Marshal Wise."

"Oh sure, sure. That'd make you Clint Adams."

"It does indeed. Did he tell you I'd be stopping by?"

"No, but with the bodies brought in the other night, I knew someone would be over in an official capacity and since it's not the marshal himself, that only leaves his right-hand man."

"I'm not exactly his right hand, but I've been helping out a bit."

"Yeah, that's what I meant. Did you want to take a look at the bodies?"

Clint felt a cringe coming on, but managed to hold it back before it showed. He wasn't exactly squeamish, but his breakfast was still sitting pleasantly in his belly and he didn't want to disturb it just yet. "No need for that," he replied. "I got a good enough look at them when they were alive."

"Oh. Then what can I do for you?"

"Actually, I was wondering if you found anything on them that was unusual. Or even if it wasn't unusual. Anything at all could be a help."

The undertaker shook his head. "Not as such. They had the clothes on their backs and not much in their pockets. It's not proper to let you have their things, but since you work for Sam and all, I could let you go through them."

"I'd appreciate it."

Turning like a man who was preparing a meal for a family get-together, the undertaker spun around and waved for Clint to follow. "Right this way, Mr. Adams. Come and have a look all you want."

Since it looked like it would take longer to do it any other way, Clint sighed and followed the undertaker into his workshop. The first thing that hit him was the smell, which reminded him of a butcher shop. Despite the fact that there was plenty of care taken to keep the workshop neat, there was simply no way to hide the scent of dead flesh.

That smell was far from unfamiliar to Clint, but it never got much easier to bear. It was the type of thing that crept right down a man's throat and stuck there for hours, if not days, later. Both bodies were lying stretched out on tables where the undertaker was cleaning them up and preparing them for burial. It wasn't a complicated process, but it wasn't hard to figure out why not too many folks wanted to do it.

"Right this way," the undertaker said while walking toward a table at the opposite end of the room. "In cases like, uh, this one I usually get rid of their clothes. If you like, I can—"

"No need for that."

"All right then. Here's their belongings. Take a look for yourself and see if anything can help you."

Much like the first time when Clint had gone through the dead men's pockets, he didn't really have any idea of what he was looking for. At least this time, he didn't feel like such a ghoul as when he'd hurried his way through to find the stagecoach schedule.

There wasn't much to look at on the table. What little money there was had been set aside, leaving nothing more than various bits and pieces including pocketknives, watches, matches, and a cigarette case.

"Actually," Clint said, "my main reason for coming here was to ask you a few questions."

"Oh?" the undertaker responded, looking as though he was surprised that anyone wanted to speak to him at all. "What're your questions?"

"First of all, do you recognize the dead men?"

"You mean the man on the right, or Larry?"

Clint glanced back to the place where the two bodies were resting. The man on the right was the one that Clint had shot. The one on the left was the one who'd been gunned down while standing upon the platform.

"Larry?" Clint said. "The man on the left's name is Larry?"

"Yes, sir. Larry Brunell. He's lived here in town for a while, but I doubt too many folks around here would recognize his face."·

"Why's that?"

"Do you know those big houses over past the business district?"

Clint nodded. He and the marshal had walked past those homes more than once. In fact, it was the spot where they both wrapped up their rounds when walking through Duskin. "Yeah. I know those places."

"Larry lived in one of the fanciest, but rarely set foot out of there. He never raised much fuss and had his food and things delivered to him, so he wasn't too well known. Kind of a . . . what's the word? A hermin?"

"You mean hermit?"

The undertaker snapped his fingers and nodded as though Clint had just won a prize. "That's the word. Hermit."

"So how did you know him?"

"I met Larry when he arranged to have a friend of his buried. We got to talking about things and had a friendly chat."

"How often did you see him?"

"Oh, just that one time."

Clint looked at the undertaker for a moment, and when he saw that no more was coming from the other man, he asked, "But you're sure it's him? He's not exactly at his best here."

The undertaker's smile slithered onto his face in a way

that sent a chill beneath Clint's skin. There wasn't any malice in the skinny man's sunken face, but the chills came all the same.

"I'm real good with faces, Mr. Adams. I see one and I can remember the name and everything else I know that goes with it. And I can spot them just as easily when they're dead. Some folks say people look different once they pass on, but not to me. We're all the same to me. All that separates us is which side of the ground we sleep on."

Hearing that, Clint had no problem figuring out where those chills had come from.

"All right then," Clint said. "Do me a favor and keep these things here in case we want to get another look."

"Will do. What about my friends over there?"

"Bury them."

The undertaker nodded and Clint left him to do his job. He couldn't remember the last time fresh air had smelled so good as when he stepped out of that parlor.

TWELVE

Clint spent the next half hour finishing up part of the rounds he'd started with Marshal Wise. It felt good to just mosey down the streets, looking for anything out of the ordinary while knowing he wouldn't find it. It was one of those few times when he got a sense of what it would be like to live like most other folks.

Most other folks didn't get shot at on a regular basis, and they sure as hell didn't go looking for the men who did the shooting. But not only did Clint make a habit out of doing just that, it was his job to do so in this case. No matter how good a walk he had, he found himself in the exact spot he knew he would when he'd started.

The houses in that section of town were large, even by Clint's standards. In his travels, he'd seen some pretty impressive homes ranging from mansions to plantation homes. The ones before him at the moment weren't the biggest he'd ever seen, but the craftsmanship in their construction was easy to see.

Where most homes were simple affairs that were lucky to have more than a few straight corners, all of these had ornate woodworking on every banister. They were well cared for as well, which said quite a bit about the town of

Duskin. It was a prosperous community where rich and poor seemed to get along fairly well.

Not all places could say that about themselves. It was just too bad that so much blood had had to come rolling down Duskin's streets when that stage had come to town. What was worse was that Clint knew there would probably be more blood on its way.

"Afternoon, Mr. Adams."

The greeting came from a well-dressed woman in her early forties with long blond hair tied back in a plain ribbon. Every time Clint saw her, she was in a fancy dress that always showed off her attractive figure. Her face was pretty and always smiling, which made her seem to glow as she looked at him. She was always friendly to him whenever her path crossed with Clint's during his rounds. As always, she nodded and smiled.

And, as always, Clint tipped his hat to her. "Hello, Anne," he said.

"Lovely day, isn't it?"

Deciding not to share the time he'd spent at the undertaker's, Clint merely nodded and gave the customary response. "Sure is. Say, could you help me out with something?"

Not only didn't Anne seem to mind Clint's question, but she was visibly pleased to stop and spend a few more moments with him. "I'll do my best."

"Do you know Larry Brunell?"

"Not very well, but he doesn't really get along with anyone too well. That is, he doesn't really come out of his house often enough to have a pleasant conversation."

Clint could detect a bit of animosity in her voice. It wasn't anything strong enough to be dislike for the reclusive man, but more of a distaste from someone used to a busier social schedule. "Do you know which house is his?" he asked.

"Why yes. It's that one over there," Anne said, pointing

toward one of the bigger houses surrounded by a white-washed fence. "Lovely place. My family lived here before it was built. Shame it had to go to someone like Lawrence." Blinking a few times, Anne cringed as if she hadn't meant to say that last part out loud.

"It's just that a house like that should be filled with children," she corrected hastily. "A family. One man rattling around in there without so much as coming out to have a word with his neighbors can't truly appreciate a home like that."

"I know what you mean," Clint said, more as a way to put an end to Anne's clumsy explanation.

"I think he's home, if you want to try and talk to him."

That one caught Clint off guard. "What?"

"He left about a week or so ago. He had some bags with him, so I imagine he was leaving town for a while. I think I saw him come home late last night. Zack was up there not too long ago, so I assume someone's home by now."

"Who's Zack?" Before he was even finished with that question, a face and name snapped into Clint's mind. "You mean Zack Michaels?"

"That's the one. Zack's one of the few people in town who Lawrence deemed worthy to talk to. They get together every now and then, but that doesn't mean Lawrence sets foot out of that house. Zack would mostly come here. They talked about gunfighters and nonsense like that." Suddenly, Anne stopped short and gave Clint an apologetic smile. "No offense."

"None taken."

Clint could just picture the upturned noses that Larry Brunell would see when he inevitably looked out of his window. Surely, Anne was one of them who watched him like a hawk while putting on the guise of a "good neighbor." Then again, he could also picture Larry's dead body lying on the undertaker's table.

"I think I'll just go have a look for myself," Clint said,

tipping his hat and then turning to walk toward the gate in the fence surrounding Larry's house.

But Anne wasn't about to let him get away from her that easily. She'd always seemed friendly enough, but now she appeared to have another purpose when she tagged along. She didn't walk all the way with him to the front door, but she watched from just a few steps behind, anxiously trying to get a look inside the house, which was probably the only one she hadn't inspected herself.

Clint knocked on the door and got no reply.

He knocked again and then leaned over to get a look through the side window. "Hello?" he shouted. "I'm here on behalf of Marshal Wise. Is anybody home?"

Anne stepped up to him tentatively. "I don't mean to intrude, but he doesn't usually answer his door."

"Are you sure he's home?"

"I saw someone walk inside, but it was late and it was awfully dark. I was in bed, but heard a door open and shut."

"And you saw Zack come over this morning?"

She nodded. "Sometimes, they go for a drink."

"Do you know where?"

Shaking her head, Anne shrugged and said, "I don't like going to saloons and such. Men get too many ideas in their heads when they get too much whiskey inside of them."

Clint had hoped she would know where else he could look, but she'd already told him a hell of a lot. "Oh, well. I was making my rounds anyway, so I might as well check out the saloons. I hope you don't think too badly of me, ma'am," he added with a wink.

"Of course not, Clint. You're a good man. I knew that the first day you decided to help Sam." She lowered her eyes and shook her head. "You must think I'm such a busybody to know so much about Lawrence."

"Not at all," Clint lied.

"It's just that I've lived right next to him for so long and have never spoken more than two words to him. If he came and went more like a normal man, I probably wouldn't even notice. As it is, he's like a bird that just pokes his beak out every couple of months."

Laughing under his breath, Clint ran his hand over the back of his neck and said, "Actually, I know how you feel. I've been here for a while and have never even met the man. I thought this house was empty."

Suddenly, Anne's eyes darted back and forth as if she was checking to see if anyone was spying on them. "If you'd like a look inside, I can arrange it."

"I never figured you for sneaking into people's houses."

"Nothing like that. My house is next door to his and you can see into his second-floor windows from my second floor. You're more than welcome to have a look for yourself if you'd like."

"What the hell," Clint said. Besides, he knew he wasn't about to disturb the house's true owner. Larry had much bigger problems than a pretty blonde peeking in through his windows.

THIRTEEN

Clint knew that Larry Brunell was dead. He'd seen the body and he'd heard what the undertaker had to say. Before he went into Anne's house, he even checked in with Sam, who'd had a chance to see the body himself. Sam recognized it as Larry Brunell, and that was all the verification that Clint needed.

There was still the matter of seeing who was going in and out of Larry's house besides Zack Michaels. With no sign of the rider that had gotten away from the platform, Clint and Sam were both of the mind to take their time and see what turned up. If someone was after something in Larry's house, they were either there, coming back soon, or long gone. Either way, there wasn't much that Clint could do about it.

Even though he would have much rather charged off to follow up whatever lead he had, the simple truth was that he had no leads. All he had were a few loose ends, and that didn't come close to telling him where to look for that killer who'd escaped from him once already.

If the years had taught him anything, it was that patience truly was a virtue. There was a time to wait and a time to run. That applied to most things in life, and it sure applied

51

to this one. Rather than chase shadows that he'd only partially glimpsed, Clint knew it was better to keep watch on the one constant in this matter that had any promise.

That constant was Larry's house. Someone had already been in there who didn't belong. Zack Michaels was a skittish type, but he was no robber and if he went into the house, it was because he thought Larry was in there as well. Clint could be wrong, but that still left him without knowing who had come into Larry's house that morning or where the hell Zack had gone.

So, instead of scouring the saloon district and hoping to cross paths with one particular needle in a haystack the size of Duskin, Clint went back to Anne's house and knocked on her door. It was late in the afternoon by the time he got back there, but there really wasn't any doubt in his mind that he would return. Part of the reason for that was the patience that he'd earned over his life. The other part was the sight that greeted him as soon as the front door opened.

"Hello again," Anne said. She was wearing the same dress that she'd had on earlier that day, but was missing a few layers. Instead of the entire ensemble, she wore only the skirt and corset under a loosely buttoned blouse. Her bustle may have been gone, but there was still plenty of curves of her own for Clint's eyes to savor.

"I was starting to think you weren't coming back," she said, filling up the doorway as though she wasn't about to let him in.

Clint shrugged and replied, "I guess I could always leave if I've worn out my welcome."

She stood there for a moment or two before the smile broke out across her face. "Don't be silly. Come on in."

Holding the door open for him, Anne waited for Clint to enter before shutting it again and turning the latch. "I've been wanting to have you over for some time. Ever since you started walking Sam's rounds, we've been wanting to show you how much we appreciate you staying."

"We?"

"Everyone in town." Anne was at the doorway to the kitchen when she stopped and looked back at him over her shoulder. "We all know Sam's needed the help, but nobody really wants to do it. Without someone like you around, there could be all sorts of mischief."

Clint moved in closer to her, but not too close. "Plenty of trouble usually happens with me around. Most times, I think folks are glad to see me go. Do you live here by yourself?"

"Normally, no. My father and sister went into Fort Laramie to visit my brother. He's stationed there."

"So they left you all alone?"

"Well, I'm not alone anymore, am I?" She let the statement hang there before turning on her heels and entering the kitchen. "I made some lemonade. Would you like some?"

"Sure."

She got some lemonade for them both and then showed him upstairs into a small sewing room. The space was kept neat and tidy, with a few small tables along the walls, and two narrow, rectangular windows covered in lace curtains. With the sun starting its drop toward the western horizon, the lace was catching just enough light to turn it a warm shade of red.

"Lawrence's house is right across this way," Anne said. "I noticed this room looks across into one of the few rooms that he actually uses."

"You seem to know an awful lot about him and his habits."

She shrugged. "I spend a lot of time in here and apart from what I see through this window, that house looks like it hasn't been lived in for years."

Clint stepped up to one of the windows and pulled some of the lace back just enough for him to peek through. He could see exactly what she was talking about the moment he laid eyes on the neighboring house. Even though there was a good deal of space in between the two houses, he could tell plenty just by taking one, quick glance.

There were plenty of windows on that side of Larry's house, but only one of them was covered in the slightest. None of the others even had their shutters closed and without anything standing in the way, it was easy to see that those rooms were practically barren.

"Has it always been like that?" Clint asked.

"It sure has."

"How long's he lived there?"

"I don't even know. That place has always been like that. In fact, my family used to think the place was completely empty. The owners would never sell it and we all figured that they were keeping it to pass on to someone else. Larry just started poking his head out of there sometime ago, and has been rattling around in there ever since."

Letting his eyes roam over the empty rooms and stark windows before settling once again on the single covered window, Clint decided that Larry Brunell gave the word "hermit" new meaning. Or, at least, he used to.

"You sure you saw someone in there?" Clint asked.

"Sure am."

"Then we'll just have to wait and see. Do you mind?"

"Not at all, Clint. Not at all."

FOURTEEN

Clint had been plenty of places throughout the years and had gotten used to a whole lot of different things. He'd been lost in deserts and chased through swamps, but none of those places seemed as awkward a fit as sitting in that small, lacy sewing room.

The first hour passed by well enough. Anne stayed right there with them, and they passed the time shooting the breeze and drinking lemonade. After that, the minutes started to crawl and Clint wondered if he wasn't wasting his time watching an empty house through lace curtains.

Then again, with his only other trail to follow being a dead man on a table and a schedule with two circles drawn on it, Clint realized he was doing the most he could do at that moment. If there was someone else taking up in the dead man's house, it could be important. If that other person was sneaking around and the cause of Zack Michaels's apparent disappearance, he knew it was definitely important.

Anne had offered him a chair, but the thing was so dainty that he felt like he would fall out of it at any second. In seconds, he'd taken up a spot standing next to the window and leaning against the wall. That way, he could look through to the next house without too much of himself being visible in case anyone else was looking back.

So far, the only movement he'd seen was caused by a stray breeze brushing a branch or leaf against the side of the house. The occasional passing shadow was his only distraction. That is, of course, until Clint felt a soft hand rub against his shoulder.

"You've been standing here a while, crouched down looking through that window," Anne said. "It doesn't look too comfortable."

"Well, that's true but I'm glad enough to be able to use your room for the moment. You don't have to worry if I'm comfortable or not."

"Don't be silly. A hostess should always be mindful of her guest. Besides," she added, moving up behind him so she could place both hands upon his shoulders, "if I didn't get my hands on you soon, I was just about to bust."

Clint turned to look behind him using just his neck. That way, he didn't have to twist out of the massage he was receiving. "Well, now, that's different. I wouldn't want you to be uncomfortable."

She leaned forward so he could see the smile on her face when she said, "And I can think of plenty of other ways to use this room."

Although he would have been lying if Clint hadn't had his own thoughts stray in this direction earlier, he hadn't quite figured Anne to be the one to take charge. It seemed that once she got behind closed doors, however, she was freed up to act however she wanted. Clint didn't mind that one bit.

After savoring the feel of her hands kneading the muscles in his back and shoulders, Clint turned around so that he was facing her. Anne didn't move in any closer as she looked at him with wide, expectant eyes. She didn't move away from him either.

It was his turn to make a move, and Clint was never one to miss an opportunity like that one.

First, he reached out to place both hands on her hips, settling his palms on the smooth curves leading down to her plump backside. After looking into her eyes for a few moments and letting the tension build a bit more, he leaned in closer until he could place his lips upon hers. Anne reacted timidly at first, kissing him as though she was still just a bit shy.

That bashfulness melted away, however, the moment Clint opened his mouth in the slightest. It was Anne who reciprocated by letting her tongue slip out to take a lingering taste of Clint's lips. She then let out a subtle breath and melted into his embrace.

Even through the skirts and layers of denim between them both, Clint could feel Anne's body squirming against him. Her arms wrapped around him and her fingers continued to work against the muscles in his back until she'd worked her way down to the base of his spine.

"I hope you don't miss anything going on out there," she whispered, giving Clint a mischievous smile.

Clint glanced to one side so he could take a quick look through the window. He could feel how much Anne wanted him as though it was a heat radiating from inside her body. He'd felt that same heat in varying degrees since the moment he'd entered her house, and had enjoyed the buildup to this moment as though it was some kind of dance.

"You're right," he replied. "Maybe I should just keep watch and you should go somewhere else so you don't distract me."

The expression on Anne's face dropped so fast that Clint half-expected to hear it pound against the floor. Her smile froze for a second before falling away, and her mouth curled into a frown that was still just a little bit sexy.

"If that's what you want," she said in a sad voice before

turning slowly away from him and moving toward the door.

Clint reached out and took hold of her wrist so quickly that it made her jump. Tightening his grip just enough to keep her from getting away, but without hurting her, he pulled her back to him. Judging by the smile that reappeared upon her face, Anne was more than happy about the situation.

"I thought you said you wanted to keep watch," she said as her eyes started wandering down along Clint's chest.

"I do, but that doesn't mean you really have to go anywhere."

"So what are you suggesting?" Anne asked, even though it showed well enough in her eyes that she had a pretty good idea.

Clint let go of her wrist and placed his hands once again upon her sides. He enjoyed moving his palms up and down over the woman's generous curves. Her body moved slightly with him, showing that she was enjoying it as well.

Eventually, Clint used his hands to guide her in front of the window with her back against the glass. Although she seemed curious as to what he was doing, she was going along with him without hesitation. "You might not be able to see much of anything with me standing here," she said.

Without a word, Clint turned her around so she was facing out the window. Now, he was the one massaging her back, and he used his hands upon her to slowly bend her down until she could place her palms on the bottom of the sill.

"Oh," she purred as she felt him move up behind her. Next, she felt his hands move down the backs of her legs just enough for him to get ahold of her skirts and hike them up. She started to say something else, but the words were lost when she felt his hands touch the bare skin of her thighs beneath her clothes.

Clint savored the slow tour he was taking of her body.

Since he wasn't saying anything to her and was out of her field of vision, all she had to go by was what she could feel. From his vantage point, Clint was enjoying the best of both worlds since he could not only see her, but could feel plenty more as well.

Every time Anne tried to talk, her breath was taken away by a new sensation brought on by the feel of Clint's fingers moving between her legs. His hand moved away just long enough for her to catch a breath, but in moments Clint was pressing his body against her from behind.

"Oh, that feels so good," she sighed, closing her eyes and no longer caring that she was being pushed against a window with just a thin layer of lace keeping her from full view of the world.

Clint moved his hands around her waist and up over her stomach, not stopping until he was able to cup her full, rounded breasts. "There now," he said, standing behind Anne, who was bent completely over the windowsill. "Now we can both see."

FIFTEEN

Part of Clint's mind was still paying attention to what was going on outside the lace-covered window. Part of him was still keeping watch on the house next door, waiting for any sign of movement coming from there. Granted, it was a very small part of him that was still on the lookout, but a part of him was nonetheless.

Most of him was paying close attention to the feel of Anne's body against his own. The movement of her hips as she ground back against him was almost as enticing as the sight of her muscles rippling in her back and her arms reaching out as she grabbed onto the windowsill and writhed back and forth against him.

Clint moved both of his hands beneath her skirt, easing it up higher until he got a good look at the smooth, rounded curve of her backside. Sure, he would have noticed something moving across the way, but it would have been because of finely honed reflexes that were always on the lookout for something that was out of place. In other words, he would have just as easily spotted a runaway train headed his direction as well at that moment. But with the sight of Anne's naked skin showing beneath her tussled clothes and the feel of her soft body pressing against his

60

groin, it might have taken something that extreme to get him to stop what he was doing.

As for Anne, she might not have noticed if the sky started falling right in front of her. Her eyes were clenched so tightly shut that the only thing she even cared about was the feel of Clint's hands on her bare skin and the waves of pleasure that slowly worked their way through her body.

Unbuckling his belt and sliding out of his jeans felt like a welcome release. Clint's erection had been getting so hard that he thought he might burst if he didn't get some satisfaction real soon. Undressing was the start of it, and real satisfaction came when he pulled Anne's panties aside so he could ease the tip of his cock between her legs.

They both let out a breathy sigh when the tip of Clint's penis brushed against the wet lips of Anne's pussy. She lowered her head, spread her legs, and gripped the sill a little tighter, waiting anxiously for his rigid length to fill her.

Clint slid easily into her and took hold of her hips with both hands so he could pull her closer while pushing deeper inside. Anne's vagina was a tight fit, so Clint eased into her slowly at first. The more he pushed, the louder Anne's moan became. Sliding out again after going in just over halfway, Clint felt Anne pushing back against him, silently begging to feel all of him inside her.

Keeping one hand on Anne's backside, Clint rubbed his other hand up and down along the small of her back as he started pumping in and out of her. Their bodies fell into an easy rhythm as he thrust his hips back and forth and Anne shifted slightly on her feet to take him in.

Her head was drooping down and her eyes were closed as she savored the feel of his cock moving inside her. Before long, she propped herself up with both hands and turned to look over her shoulder. The sight of Clint working to enter her from behind sent another wave of pleasure through her, making her pussy even wetter than it already was.

Clint saw her looking at him and met her gaze as he

took hold of her hips with both hands again and pumped into her with a strong push of his hips. Although the force of his thrust was a surprise, it was certainly a welcome one and Anne was unable to keep the groan from escaping her lips.

The sound of her voice filled the room for a moment, followed by the quickening rhythm of their bodies meeting as Clint pounded into her again and again. Anne kept her eyes on him and spread her legs apart a little more, allowing him to glide effortlessly between them.

Clint's rigid penis slipped inside her again and again, rubbing against her clitoris and bringing her that much closer to her climax. Her breaths were coming in shallow bursts now, and when she felt Clint's hands settle upon her shoulders, she knew it wouldn't be much longer before her orgasm would rush through her entire body.

Using his hold upon her shoulders to guide his thrusts even more, Clint pumped his hips back and forth until Anne was fighting to keep from screaming with the orgasm he gave her. The lips of her pussy tightened around him, making it feel that much better when he slowed his rhythm down and savored the smooth way his cock glided between her legs.

After a few moments, Anne was able to see straight again and she pulled in a few deep breaths. Although Clint was still inside her, he was keeping still and reaching around to cup her breasts with both hands. The heavy weight of them filled his palms, and he could feel her erect nipples through the material of her dress.

Feeling her pull away from him, Clint let her disengage for a moment so she could turn around and face him.

"Don't worry," she said in a breathy whisper. "We're not done yet. I just think you'll have to keep watch for the both of us while I tend to better things." With that, Anne hopped up onto the sill, which was just wide enough for her to sit upon.

Giving Clint a sexy smile, she pulled her skirt up and spread her legs so he could see the thatch of hair between them as well as her glistening pink lips. Once she reached down with one hand to spread her pussy open a little for him, Clint felt his erection become even harder, and he didn't even try to hold off before plunging it inside her once more.

Clint felt her legs wrap tightly around him, soon to be followed by her arms, which cinched in around the back of his neck. With her holding on to him like that, he was free to start a whole new rhythm. This time, as he slid in and out of her, he could feel and hear her breaths in his ear since her head was resting on his shoulder.

With both hands grasping her buttocks, Clint felt her body tremble with a second climax. Her breathing quickened and she started moaning his name into his ear as her pleasure reached its peak. Clint felt his body responding to all of that, and soon he was ready to explode inside her. As he did, he picked her up off the sill and pumped once more into her.

Suddenly, he stopped.

"What's wrong?" Anne asked breathlessly.

Looking across into the next house, Clint replied, "I think we're the ones being watched."

SIXTEEN

Clint's heart was still slamming in his chest after the time he'd had with Anne in her sewing room. Pulling on his clothes and making sure all the buckles and buttons had been fastened properly, Clint cinched his gun belt around his waist and checked once more out the window.

Although the figure he'd seen there before was no longer looking back at him, he was certain of what he'd seen only a minute or two ago. There had been a face looking through one of the windows of a room that was supposedly empty. That face had pulled back into the darkness as soon as Clint spotted it.

"What is it, Clint?" Anne asked, getting herself together and straightening out her dress. "Is something wrong? Is someone watching us?"

When Clint looked out the window this time, Anne looked as well. Neither one of them saw anything, but that didn't mean there nothing was there.

Clint's mind was racing in several directions. While pulling his clothes back on and getting the Colt back to where he could reach it, he hadn't said much of anything. The more he stayed silent, the more nervous Anne became.

Finally, she reached out and took hold of him by the arm, forcing him to look straight at her.

"Tell me what's wrong," she demanded.

That snapped Clint out of his own thoughts and caused him to take a moment to see things from her perspective. "Sorry to spook you like that," he told her, "but I'm going to have to get a look over there for myself."

"Did you see someone in the window? Was it Lawrence?"

"I did see someone, but I'm not sure who it was." He thought about breaking the news to her about Larry's death, but decided that would just add fuel to the fire. For the moment, he just needed to get over to that house and see things for himself. Every second he wasted was giving whoever it was more of a chance to get away.

"Please, Anne, just stay here and wait for me to come back. It's probably nothing, but I just need to get a look for myself. All right?"

With her nerves calmed somewhat, Anne nodded. "All right. Should I find Marshal Wise?"

"No, not just yet. If you hear any commotion over there, don't try to get him either. Just stay put until I come to get you."

The nerves that had just been settled suddenly bunched up into a knot when Anne heard that last part. "What kind of commotion? What's going on? Clint, I'm getting scared."

"Don't be scared. I'll come back before you know I'm gone. It's probably nothing anyway." Clint gave her a quick kiss and headed for the door. He knew Anne would be a wreck until he returned, but he couldn't wait one more second. If the man he'd spotted was involved in Larry's death, he should have had the sense to leave once he saw he'd been discovered.

Then again, most killers couldn't be accused of having good sense.

• • •

It was early evening and the stars were all making their appearance overhead. Without so much as a cloud in the sky, the pale light shining down was enough to allow Clint to move quickly from one house to another. Even though he was only going to the neighboring home, there was quite a bit of property to cover as well as a fence standing in his way.

With most of Larry's windows open or bare altogether, Clint had to be real careful in making his approach to the house. If there was someone inside, that person could be watching him from any of those windows. Then again, there was also the chance that the house was empty and the person was gone, or that Clint had just imagined the entire thing.

In a way, being tricked by a reflection or jumpy nerves would have been a relief. That would mean that there was still nothing in that house and that Larry had just been shot for some reason that would never be uncovered. As comforting as that would have been in many ways, Clint knew damn well that he shouldn't wait for that to be the case. He'd come to trust his instincts too well for them to fail him when he was specifically counting on them.

All of this ran through his mind as Clint ran across Anne's yard, hopped the fence, and approached Larry's house from the side opposite the one he'd been watching. As he moved, his senses took in everything that was going on around him.

He heard the rustle of the wind.

He felt every slope of the ground beneath his feet.

And he saw the familiar Appaloosa tethered to a tree in a dark corner of the backyard.

SEVENTEEN

There was no mistaking that Appaloosa. Anyone with an eye for horses would have spotted the coloring of that breed, which was given away by the black and white spotted marks on its rump. More than that, however, Clint had been picturing that specific horse in his mind ever since it had left him in the dust back on that platform.

All this time, Clint had been hoping to catch up with that horse one way or another. Well, it looked like this was his lucky night in more ways than just his encounter with Anne next door.

From where he was, Clint could tell the horse was sleeping. Its head was hanging down low and its sides moved with a slow, heavy rhythm like a pair of bellows slowly churning a fire. Being careful not to wake the animal, Clint kept his distance while closing in on the house itself. He knew a place that size had to have more than just a front and back door, and quickly found a narrow side entrance.

The closer he got to that house, the more he wanted to hurry up and get inside. Clint could feel his stomach clenching with the certainty that he was still close to losing whoever was inside. Most of that came from thinking so much about tracking down that killer, and plenty of that came from the simple fact that Clint didn't like to lose.

It was a straightforward thing and natural enough in any gambler. Despite the fact that letting a few losses come and go was a natural part of things, that didn't mean that he had to like it. Much like poker, the rest of life was filled with bluffs, wins, and losses. Having those men ride up and kill someone in front of Clint was only the first hand to be dealt. Since then, Clint had been forced to sit out altogether.

Well, that had just changed. Now that he'd finally been dealt the next hand, he was anxious to play it through. He stopped and took a breath before proceeding, though, just to make sure he didn't tip his hand.

That little pause, it turned out, made all the difference.

In the time that Clint took to take a breath before opening that narrow side door, he heard something like muted bumps coming from within the house. Half a second later, the door directly in front of him was pulled open and he came face-to-face with a short man dressed in clothes that still looked rumpled after a long ride.

The man's face was sprouting thick stubble and his mouth was set in a thin, determined line. That mouth dropped open a bit when he was forced to stop short before running straight into Clint. His cold, dark eyes widened for a moment before narrowing again with newfound resolve.

That moment seemed to freeze for the both of them. Clint snapped back into motion first by reaching out with one hand to try and get ahold of the man's wrist. But the figure in the doorway wasn't far behind, and turned out to have a decent amount of speed himself.

Clint's fingers had just started to close around the man's wrist when the man pulled his arm back. A jolt of strength along with a quick twist was all he needed to break free of Clint's grasp. Baring his teeth while letting out a snarling breath, the man balled up his fist and sent that same arm straight back at Clint's face.

Although he saw the punch coming, Clint was too close to do much about it, and caught the fist on his chin. He did manage to roll with the blow a little bit, and that was all that kept him from getting knocked back or his jaw broken altogether. When he twisted back around to look into the doorway, Clint was ready for anything.

The man's lips were curled in a vicious smile. Like an animal that had smelled blood, he couldn't help following up his punch with another one hot on its heels. This time, he sent his other hand toward Clint's jaw, determined to knock the sense out of Clint's skull.

All that punch managed to do was create a gust of wind just outside the doorway because Clint had ducked clean beneath it. Once the punch had sailed over his head, Clint straightened up and used the motion of his body and legs to add power to his own jab to the man's gut.

The impact of Clint's punch sounded like a sledgehammer landing in the room just inside the narrow doorway. The force of it staggered the man and caused him to take a few wobbly steps back into the house. Clint was right behind him, and even reached back to pull the door shut once he was inside.

"Who are you?" Clint asked. "What are you doing here?"

Spitting out a wad of spit and blood, the man snarled, "I own this house!"

"Bullshit. The man who owns this house is laying stretched out in the undertaker's workshop."

That brought a cruel smile to the man's face. It was all Clint could do to keep from knocking that smile completely off his skull with his bare hands.

"One more chance," Clint warned. "Start telling me what I want to know or—"

"Or what?" the man challenged. "You'll hurt me? You'll need to find me first."

With that, the man turned his back on Clint and ran further into the house. Clint's first instinct was to follow, but he stopped when he noticed that he was standing in almost complete darkness.

The room he was in was about the size of a large closet, and was probably some kind of mud room meant to hold coats and shoes before going further into the building. There was just enough light filtering in for Clint to make out the closest two walls on either side of him. After that, the pale light from the night sky died off and no matter how adjusted to the dark his eyes had gotten, there was no way to see much more.

Still feeling the sting of the punch that had bounced off the side of his face, Clint focused on the sound of footsteps coming from deeper inside the house, and set off into the darkness. Those footsteps were moving quickly inside and were obviously circling around to try to flank Clint's position.

"You shoulda stayed out of this, Gunsmith," the man said from somewhere not too far away. "It didn't concern you."

"I got concerned as soon as that man was killed right in front of me," Clint replied, using the sound of his voice to cover his footsteps.

"Yeah, well, it's a shame that concern of yours is gonna get you killed."

The shot blasted through the house and lit up the man's face in a sudden, brilliant flash.

EIGHTEEN

The shot rattled Clint right down to the core because it was the exact thing he'd been hoping not to hear. Since the other man was moving so quickly in the dark, it was obvious that he was already more than familiar with the layout of the house. That meant that he had the advantage and that Clint was treading on very dangerous ground.

The bullet cut through the air like a hornet and hissed toward Clint with deadly rage. He heard the lead screaming toward him, but there was little more he could do than drop down and hope for the best. Thankfully, either Clint's reflexes were still fast enough to save his life, or the man who'd pulled the trigger wasn't so sure of his target after all.

In the blink of an eye, the bullet had torn down its path and found its final resting place. That place just happened to be in the wall just a few inches from where Clint had been standing moments ago. There was no way for him to know just how close the bullet had come and no reason for Clint to dwell on it. All he cared about was that it had missed and now it was time to make the man wish he'd never pulled that trigger.

Crouching low and holding close to the floor, Clint pushed forward with both legs to send himself into a forward roll. It wasn't anything pretty, but it served the purpose of getting him away from the doorway and out of the line of fire. In his mind's eye, he could still see where that flash of gunfire had come from, and he made sure to put himself out of that line of fire.

When Clint came to a stop, he bumped slightly against a wall, and took a moment to steady himself in his new spot. He didn't remember drawing the Colt, but the modified pistol was in his hand all the same and ready to return fire.

"Where you at, Gunsmith?" the man sneered. "The big man hiding after one little shot?"

Clint was a long way past being goaded by simple taunts like that. In fact, he was thankful for them because they gave him time to take a moment and see where he was. In that moment, Clint found out a hell of a lot. First of all, he realized that the man who'd been shooting at him couldn't see in the dark.

There were a few lanterns here and there, giving off just enough light to give the room a dim glow. Although those few lanterns added mostly shadows, they still made it possible to move about without breaking one's neck.

Secondly, Clint realized that nobody had been in that house for some time. At least, nobody had been in that room, which appeared to be the main entry room. The dim, flickering light coming off the lanterns showed the gritty textures that were all covered with thick layers of dust. Once his eyes had focused, Clint could even see footsteps in that dust, as though the floor was covered with freshly fallen snow.

The freshest of those tracks led to the bottom of a flight of stairs. Clint didn't have to see any more than that to know that the man had taken those stairs to get to the higher ground. In fact, Clint could still see that flash of gunfire coming at him from that vantage point.

"Hey, Gunsmith," came the now-familiar voice. "Where you hidin'?"

Having taken his time to get his bearings, Clint was now ready to get back on the move. Gripping the Colt in one hand, he kept the weapon ready as he started creeping toward the stairs with his back pressed against the wall.

Every footstep scraped along the dirty floor, sounding like thunder in his ears. He knew his steps weren't really that loud, but when he wanted to be quiet above all else, any noise he made sent a chill down his back.

Stopping before rounding the corner, Clint closed his eyes and focused all his attention on what his ears could tell him. He knew exactly what he wanted to hear, and it was the same sound that he'd been making himself. Now that he was standing still, however, he knew that the scraping footsteps he heard had to belong to the man he was after.

This time, when he heard that sound, Clint's reaction was a whole lot different. A victorious grin eased onto his face, and he readied himself for the man to come around the corner after slinking down those stairs.

Clint's celebration was short-lived, however, because the light footsteps he'd been listening to stopped. For a moment, Clint wondered if the man was able to see better in the dark than he'd realized. There was also the possibility that there was another man hiding somewhere in the shadows and that Clint was moving directly into an ambush.

Rather than sit rooted to the spot while pondering all the possibilities, Clint acted on whatever information he had. Those footsteps were still gone, but another sound had taken their place. This one was more of a scraping, like someone moving furniture or a boot being dragged against solid wood.

Clint listened for another moment while moving toward the base of the stairs. All of his senses were stretching out to grab onto anything they could find. Anything at all. All he got was that scraping, which was coming from above him and to one side, but could have been any number of movements coming from his quarry.

Before rounding the bend and charging up the stairs, Clint pressed back against the wall built to close the gap beneath the steps. He took a deep breath and rested his head against the wall as well, just to give himself a moment to see or hear anything else before pushing on.

Lives were decided in moments like those, along with plenty of deaths. Men who ignored those precious seconds wound up playing into someone else's hand, which was usually the last mistake of their lives. Clint believed in using those moments, even when they stretched his nerves to their limits.

In this particular moment, he heard that scraping sound once more. This time, with his head against the wall, he could hear something else that made all the difference. Apart from the scraping, he heard a subtle tap. That was all he needed to picture what was causing the sounds.

Until now, he thought it was just the man making his way down the stairs to get to him or just get a better position. Clint changed his mind now, however, and rather than look toward the base of the stairs or around that corner, he looked straight up.

The man was right there above him. After having climbed up onto the banister, he'd managed to get his footing secure enough to stand with both feet on the rail. Crouching low with arms outstretched and gun in hand, he looked like a gargoyle carved into the side of an old church.

The sight was so odd that it took Clint a moment to react to it. His reflexes were good enough to get him moving a fraction of a second after the man started dropping down toward him. Clint pushed back with one foot and hopped out of the spot where he'd been standing. The man landed and kept his feet planted, displaying the same balance that had kept him from toppling off the banister moments ago.

Although impressed by the display, Clint wasn't about to let himself be caught off guard. Now that he knew the kind of man he was dealing with, Clint entered the fray by thrusting his left fist out in a quick, short jab to the stomach.

The man twisted away to deflect most of the blow, but caught a few knuckles in his ribs. A gust of breath was forced from his lungs, but he still managed to follow up with a swing of his own. He lashed out with his gun hand, twisting his fist so he could crack Clint's skull with the butt of his pistol.

In the blink of an eye, Clint decided what to do and was already moving in that direction. A flicker of motion was all it took for him to holster the Colt. From there, he crossed both arms over his head to catch the incoming blow in a solid grip.

The man had his other hand free, however, and when Clint saw the knife he'd drawn with that free hand, it was almost too late to do anything about it.

NINETEEN

Clint reacted as though he'd known the knife was on its way the entire time. His speed came from more than just quick reflexes. It came from the fact that he didn't stop to question those reflexes before letting them take him over.

The blood pounded through him like steam through an engine, giving him the power to grab hold of the man's wrist even tighter while twisting his body in a quick semicircle to allow the blade to graze along his stomach rather than stab through it. Even though the motion took a fraction of a second to complete, it left him breathless.

Clint could feel blood trickling down his stomach, but ignored the twinge of pain accompanying the cut. Still moving with the momentum he'd built up, he twisted the man's wrist even more while tugging his arm straight down toward the floor.

The man grunted with the effort of trying to get his arm free from Clint's grasp, but was unable to move anywhere but the way Clint wanted him to move. Before he knew what was going on, the man was being dragged down and a sharp pain was shooting throughout his entire right side. Before he felt his bones start to snap, he let go of his pistol and turned himself around to accommodate Clint's lead.

The pistol hit the floor and thumped to one side. Clint felt the gun drop against his boot, so he kicked it away with a quick motion. As soon as the man's back hit the floor, he was curling his legs up close to his chest so he could snap them straight out in a brutal double kick.

It wasn't a fancy move by any means, but it certainly got the job done. Clint still had both hands occupied when the man's heels came straight toward him. As quick as Clint's reflexes might have been, there was no way for him to dodge those feet, and twisting away from them would only have resulted in broken ribs instead of a sore stomach.

Even though Clint's muscles clenched instinctively, his breath was still knocked out of him when those kicks landed. The shadows seemed to dim a bit more as his vision clouded and his chest lit up with a pain that felt like fire inside him. Clint staggered back and sucked some more air into his lungs, which gave the man on the floor a chance to recover as well.

Since his gun had been knocked away, the man was only left holding his blade. He was wary of getting close enough to stab at Clint again, so he cocked his arm back and prepared to throw it instead.

Clint saw that movement and reacted instantly to it. His hand flashed down to his holster and wrapped around the grip of his Colt. Just as the muscles in the man's arms were tensing in preparation to throw the knife, Clint had cleared leather and was showing his target the business end of its barrel.

"Drop it," Clint said in a cold, even tone. "Now."

Seeing he was beaten, the man let out a curse under his breath and allowed the blade to slip from his fingers. The knife clattered on the floor, which filled the mostly empty house with the sound of metal against wood.

Taking a step back, Clint kept the Colt aimed at the other man. "Sit up." When the man started to get to his feet, Clint shook his head and added, "I said sit up, not stand. Sit with your back against that wall."

The man did what he was told, crossing his arms over his chest.

Both men were dirty and battered, but neither of them paid a bit of mind to their wounds. Clint felt a stabbing pain every time he drew a breath, and could tell that one side of his face was already starting to swell. The man beneath him looked also the worse for wear.

"So you know who I am," Clint said. "Just who the hell are you?"

"Larry's cousin. That's why I made myself at home in this house. You're the intruder here."

"Is that so? And why would Larry's cousin want to kill Larry himself?"

The man shrugged and gave Clint a smug, shit-eating grin. "You don't know I killed anyone. You busted into my house, so I tried to get you out. A man's got the right to protect his property, don't he?"

Clint could tell this was going nowhere. Just as he was about to start in on a new tactic, he heard a sound coming from somewhere deeper within the house.

". . . hello? Anyone there?" came a weak, uncertain voice.

Clint's eyes stayed on the man in front of him, but his brain was already narrowing down where that voice could have come from. "Who is that?" Clint asked the man on the floor.

All he got in response was that same smirk, followed up with a shrug.

"You'd best start talking," Clint said.

"Or what? If you were gonna shoot, you woulda done so by now. And if you mean to lock me up, then you'll do that no matter what I say or don't say."

"You think you're smart?"

"Maybe, maybe not, but I know a lawdog when I see

one. Lawdogs don't gun down helpless men no matter how much they want to." When he said those last couple words, the man put in a special kind of emphasis that made Clint want nothing more than to pull his trigger.

Now, it was Clint who shrugged. "Good point. All right then, since Sam sent me in here to take care of this problem, I'll just take care of it."

The man's smirk faded a bit. "You bringin' me in?"

"No," Clint replied while raising his Colt. "I'm shooting you before you shoot me. Self-defense, pure and simple, and nobody will say any different."

"You can't do that," the man said as he started squirming.

"Oh, no? Why shouldn't I? You said yourself that I wanted to gun you down."

The man's eyes darted back and forth as he tried desperately to come up with something to save his skin. Before he could say anything, the air was filled with the slam of a door being opened and the rush of soft, quick footsteps over the dusty floor.

Clint glanced back to see a figure rushing toward him. At that same moment, he saw the man on the floor jump to his feet and start moving for the closest batch of thick shadows. There was a choice that needed to be made and Clint had less than a second to make it.

TWENTY

The voice upstairs called down again in desperation.

Besides that, Clint could hear the new footsteps coming from the back of the house as well as the shuffling of the man on the floor in front of him. With the concern about an ambush still fresh in his mind, Clint took a quick look behind him and prepared to take a shot at whoever was charging at him from the shadows.

This time, Clint's reflexes were quick enough to keep him from pulling the trigger rather than taking a shot when Anne came rushing into the large foyer. The instant he saw her face, Clint turned back around and dropped to one knee in preparation for whatever the other man had in store for him.

Clint caught the man in mid-stretch, reaching for the gun that had been kicked out of his reach. Less than two inches from the weapon's grip, the man froze once he saw that he was now once again in Clint's line of fire.

"Dammit, Anne, I told you to stay put," Clint said in a voice that was a bit rougher than he'd intended.

Although she'd stopped the moment she saw what was happening in the large room, Anne was still shifting nervously from one foot to another. "I know, Clint, but I had to come over here to tell you that . . ."

Her words faded away, but Clint refused to take his eyes off of the man he had at gunpoint. "Tell me what?" he asked. "You can go ahead and say what you wanted to say."

"She wanted to tell you to let Ed go."

The response was a voice that Clint didn't recognize. It didn't come from the man in front of him, and it sure as hell didn't come out of Anne. Rather than look away from his target, Clint stepped sideways so he could keep the man on the floor in the corner of his eye while taking a look at the newest arrival.

The flickering light from the few lanterns scattered about may have been dim, but it was enough to glint off the iron being pointed at Anne's head. Clint spotted the gun aimed at her and felt his stomach clench.

"And who are you?" Clint asked, his voice sounding calm and in total control. "If I knew there'd be so many people in this house, I would've thought someone might have cleaned up a bit."

The man holding the gun on Anne was mostly obscured in shadow. There simply wasn't much more of him to see apart from his hand and a sliver of his face. Despite the fact that he couldn't see much of the newest arrival, Clint could tell a whole lot by the one eye illuminated in the pale light.

"You got three seconds before I pull this trigger, Adams," the man behind Anne said. "You can either spend them making conversation or you can do what I asked and maybe save this bitch's life."

The seconds ticked by. Clint felt them pass just as surely as if he could hear a clock's gears echoing throughout the room. He took a better look at what little he could see, which was enough for Clint to decide that the other man wasn't bluffing.

With half a second to spare, Clint holstered his Colt and

held his hands out to either side. "There," he said. "Is that better?"

"Get out of here, Ed," the man said from the shadows.

Ed backed away from where Clint had him pinned down and walked toward the door. "If you know what's good for you, you'll leave this alone," Ed told Clint. "I got the drop on you once and I can do it again." With that said, he left the house and shut the door behind him.

Clint turned toward Anne and the man still holding her at gunpoint. "All right then. Are you going to hold up your end of the bargain?"

After a few moments of silence, which seemed to drag on for an hour or so, the man stepped back just enough for him to be completely out of the flickering light. Anne felt a nudge and that was all she needed to rush forward and into Clint's arms.

"Stay out of this, Adams," the man said from the darkness. "You've been left out until now as a courtesy. If you stick your nose in any further, that courtesy will be pulled right out from under you. Believe me, you don't want that to happen."

"It would help if I knew what I was supposed to be keeping clear of."

"Don't try to soak me for information. Just forget about what happened here. Forget about Larry Brunell and forget about any sad stories that lady told you about her brother. None of it concerns you and—"

"Yeah, yeah," Clint interrupted. "And if I make it my concern it'll be the last mistake I make."

"Something like that."

Those words drifted through the air like smoke, soon to be followed by the light touch of boots against the floor as the man made his exit through the same door he'd used to get in.

Anne started to say something as she tightened her hold around Clint, but he silenced her with a quick shake of his head. Clint had every ounce of his attention focused on finding another sound that didn't belong. All he heard was the rustle of wind against the shutters and Anne's frantic breathing.

Clint was fairly certain that both men had gone, but he wasn't about to bet on it until he could examine every inch of that house. Since he didn't want to waste that much time, he motioned for Anne to keep quiet and took her by the hand as he moved quickly toward the stairs. His other hand stayed close to the Colt at his side, ready to clear leather at a moment's notice.

"Is there anyone there?" the voice from upstairs called out yet again. "Oh, God," it said quietly. "Oh, God, oh, God."

Clint followed the sound of the other person's pleading and groaning until it led him to a small room next to one of the few in the house that were actually furnished and lived in. As he made his way to the source of that voice, Clint was expecting a lot of things.

Even so, what he found caused him to stop short for a moment and wonder what the hell he'd stumbled into this time.

TWENTY-ONE

The first thing Clint saw in that room was blood.

In fact, there was so much blood that he needed a moment or two to take it in before he got himself to move forward. He actually only stood by for a second before running forward and rushing to the person who had been calling out every so often in a weak, trembling voice.

"Jesus, Zack, what the hell happened to you?" Clint asked as he entered the room and hurried to the man bleeding there.

Zack looked at him as if he wasn't quite sure what he was seeing. He was tied to a chair in the corner that was farthest from the window. By the looks of it, the room had been used as Larry's own bedroom. There was a single dresser as well as a cot with a few blankets tossed over it. The only other furniture in there was the chair that Zack was bound to.

The man's arms and legs were tied to the chair with several loops of rope. There was something dangling around his neck that looked as if it had been used as a gag, but had since fallen out of Zack's mouth. Clint noticed all of this first simply because the rest of it was too grisly for him to consider without taking a moment to brace himself.

One thing was for certain. Whoever had gone to work on Zack surely knew how to use a knife. There were slashes across his face and arms that were deep enough to bleed, but not serious enough to do more than that. Those were obviously only the beginning however, with the real work being what was done to his hands and legs.

As he set about untying the ropes, Clint got a closer look at Zack's injuries. His left hand was nothing more than bloody meat hanging off the end of his arm. The flesh had been carved away in large strips as if it had been whittled off the bone. There wasn't much left of his fingers to speak of, apart from some smaller bones protruding from more flayed skin and tissue.

Compared to the left one, Zack's right hand was in fairly good condition. The only problem was that it was resting on the floor about two feet away from the chair where he was sitting.

Clint got the last of the ropes off of Zack, and was ready to catch him when the man fell over. Zack's skin was pale and it was a miracle that he even had the energy left to keep his eyes open. Then again, the pain coursing through his body was more than enough to keep him awake through the loss of blood.

"Wha . . . what's going on?" Zack wheezed. "Is that you, Clint?"

"Yeah, Zack. It's me." Clint helped Zack up off the chair and then lifted him onto his feet. "We need to get out of here. Think you can make it if I help you?"

"Out of . . . here? Yes. Please . . . get me . . . home."

"Let's just get you out of this house for the time being. After we get you bandaged up, we'll get you right home."

Zack's head lolled forward and when he pulled it back again, he was smiling vaguely. "Bandaged up? Hope so."

"We'll get you to the . . ." Clint stopped himself before completing that sentence. Zack did plenty of things in Duskin, and one of them was acting as the town's doctor.

Clint's eyes widened and he looked to Anne for a suggestion to what they could do next.

That look was all she needed to see to know what Clint was thinking. The fear that had been on her face dissolved, and she rushed forward to help carry Zack. "Let's get him to my house. After that, we can send for Jeremy Larson. He knows a thing or two about medicine."

"Good. Let's just get the hell out of here," Clint said.

With Clint under one of Zack's arms and Anne under the second, they managed to carry the wounded man out of the room, down the stairs, and out of the house in minutes. Their footsteps made wet, squishing sounds as they tracked through the blood in the room where Zack had been found. Even after they'd gone downstairs, there was enough blood on the bottoms of their feet to make it still sound as though they were walking in mud.

The three of them moved through the house quickly, but it still seemed to take forever for them to get outside. Before they reached the door, Anne's voice cut through the wet shuffle of feet and the roar of blood going through all of their ears.

"Do you think they're really gone, Clint?" she asked. "Do you think they might be waiting for us?"

"I doubt they're that stupid," Clint replied. "Since I'd blast them out of their boots the first time I laid eyes on them."

With that grim promise fresh in the air, the trio made their way out of the house and across to Anne's home. Clint took a quick look over to where he'd spotted that Appaloosa before, figuring the horse would be gone. He was correct. The yard now seemed every bit as empty as the house itself.

Clint could feel the warmth of Zack's blood soaking into his clothes where the man's arms were resting. After what had been done to the man, Clint wished he could do something to ease his pain before moving him. But the most important thing, he knew, was to get Zack somewhere safe. He could worry about the rest later.

Despite the agony flooding most of his body and the cold numbness that embraced the rest, Zack still tried to walk rather than dangle between Clint and Anne. His boots had been taken from him and his feet were a bloody mess, but he was already in too much pain to notice a bit more.

Once they were back on Anne's property, they all felt a little more at ease. Anne felt that way because she was at home. Zack was grateful to be anywhere but tied to that chair. As for Clint, he took a few easier breaths simply because he knew that if those others were going to make another try at them, they would have done so when they had their hands full with the wounded man.

That was simply how men like that thought.

It was how animals thought.

And that was exactly how Clint thought of men who would do something like what had been done to Zack. They were animals and from that moment on, Clint had every intention of hunting them like animals.

TWENTY-TWO

Since there was still the possibility of there being a danger from those gunmen, Clint was the one to go and fetch Jeremy Larson. It was easy enough to find the young man since he was still tending to some patients at Zack Michaels's office. When Clint burst through the door covered in someone else's blood, he didn't have one bit of trouble in getting Jeremy to follow him.

By the time they got to Anne's, Zack had passed out. His breathing shook his entire body and the blood had dried to a thick crust at the ends of his arms and legs. Clint left the room once he saw that Jeremy was able to treat Zack's wounds.

Stepping out of the house to get a breath of fresh air, Clint started walking toward the gate in Anne's fence. He soon heard footsteps rushing up to meet him. After all the steps he'd been listening to over the last couple of hours, Clint had no trouble picking out who these belonged to.

They stopped behind him, just short of entering Clint's field of vision. Without turning around, Clint asked, "What is it, Anne?"

Her voice was hesitant and more than a little shaky. "I'm sorry, Clint. I'm so sorry."

"Sorry for what?"

"If I would've just stayed put, none of this would have happened."

Clint turned around and started to answer. When he saw the hurt in her eyes, he wrapped his arms around her before saying a word. She melted against him and almost broke down into tears. Finally, he held her at arm's length so he could look straight into her eyes.

"You didn't do anything wrong," he told her. "Whatever happened had already happened before you got there."

"Yeah, but if I wasn't there, those men might not have gotten away."

"And if you weren't there, I might not have ever known that second gunman was there. Whether you meant to or not, you flushed him out and forced their hand before they got a chance to pick me off from the shadows."

That seemed to make her feel a bit better, but not much. At the very least, Anne wasn't going to cry any longer. "Do you think they're still there?" she asked, glancing in the direction of Larry's house.

"No."

"Do you know who they are?"

That question cut right to the core of what was still gnawing away at the bottom of Clint's gut. "No," he said. "But I am a few steps closer."

"Really? Did you recognize one of them? They sure seemed to know who you are."

"Not to sound too full of myself, but a lot of people know who I am. Most of what they heard isn't exactly true, but they know my name well enough. Actually, it wasn't so much what I saw, but what I heard. That man that held the gun on you told me to forget about Larry and to forget about anything you might have said about your brother. That tells me right there that he considers those things to be important."

"Lawrence isn't in any shape to talk right now, but Jeremy said he should be able to hang on."

"So what about your brother?" Clint asked. "You didn't really say much of anything to me about him except that he wasn't here."

"That's right. He's stationed at Fort Laramie."

Clint nodded, trying to fit together what he'd heard while also trying to pull up anything he could remember that could even vaguely connect them. "What's your brother's name?"

"Ken Mortenson."

Clint didn't recognize the name right away, but thought it over for a second to see if it might trigger anything. It didn't. "And what does he do at Fort Laramie?"

"He's a master sergeant."

"Do you know what his duties are?"

She shrugged and answered, "He's told me once or twice, but I never really seem to remember the details. I do know that he's in charge of keeping records or something regarding supplies."

That sparked something in Clint's head. "What kind of supplies?"

"Clothes, I guess. Maybe boots and the like."

"Does he work with the payroll?"

"Could be."

"What about weapons?"

When Clint saw the way Anne's face lit up at the sound of that question, his stomach knotted up even more.

"He does handle weapons," she said with certainty. "I recall him telling me that specifically because he goes on and on in his letters about such-and-such a new-model rifle or some other kind of gun. It doesn't make a whole lot of sense to me, but he gets worked up about those kinds of things."

It made sense to Clint, but in a way that made him realize things might be a bit more involved than just the death of one man on a stagecoach loading platform.

"Does that help you?" she asked.

Clint forced himself to smile and nod as though things hadn't just gone from bad to worse. "Yeah, Anne. That helps me a lot. Do you recall him mentioning anything that stands out as strange?"

"Strange? Like what?"

"I don't know. Anyone giving him any trouble, something he might have noticed, or just anything that didn't fit with everything else he normally talked about?"

Anne took a breath and closed her eyes as if she was picturing every letter in her mind and recalling every conversation. Finally, she opened her eyes and gave Clint another shrug. "I can't think of anything. I'm sorry."

"Let's not start that again," Clint said gently. "If you do think of anything once things calm down, let me know." With that, he gave her a quick kiss on the cheek and started walking away from the house.

"Where are you going?" she called out after him.

"I need to find Sam and tell him what happened. I'll send someone to stay here with you before anything else, though."

Nodding, Anne wrapped her arms tightly around herself and said, "Please take care of yourself."

"I will." Despite the confidence in his voice, Clint knew that small task would be much easier said than done.

TWENTY-THREE

Clint caught up with Marshal Wise even before he made it back to the lawman's office. The words came so quickly from Clint's mouth that he barely even recalled asking the marshal to send someone over to Anne's house to act as a guard. Wise may have been short on deputies, but he had a few young men that he used to back him up under certain circumstances. The boys weren't much more than hired guns working for the right side of the law, but they were all that was required to fit Clint's request.

Once two such guards had been dispatched, Clint and Sam headed back to the marshal's office, where they could talk. Once there, Clint headed straight for the collection of wanted posters kept in a battered leather cover on Sam's desk.

"What the hell happened over there, Clint?" Sam asked. "You look like you've been through a war."

Clint didn't have to look down at his clothes to know they were dirty, rumpled, and covered in blood. "Not quite a war, but you may not be too far off the mark."

Sam pulled out a chair and dropped himself into it. "I don't like the sound of that."

"Neither do I, but it's there all the same."

As Clint flipped through the wanted notices, he told Sam about what had happened at Larry Brunell's house. The marshal listened without much reaction so as not to interrupt Clint before he was through. Once the account was finished, Sam stood up and let out a breath as if he'd been the one to make it through the fight.

"Jesus, Clint, I wish I could've been there to help."

"Believe me, if I would've known what might happen, I would have been the first one to ask for some backup. None of us knew what was coming, so let's just leave it at that."

"You recognize either of the men that were there?"

Clint shook his head and sped through the last couple of sheets in the book. "This is the second time I've been through this damn thing and I still don't see any familiar faces in here."

"And you said Anne's brother Kenny has something to do with this?"

"Yeah. I can't say whether or not he's into some bad business or just wrapped up with some bad men, but he's definitely involved. Do you know anything about him?"

"Just that he's a soldier. Anne's brought him up once or twice, but only to brag about how nice he looks in his uniform. Tell you the truth, sometimes she talks so much about useless things that I don't pay her too much mind."

A smile snuck onto Clint's face, and it felt strange for him to have it there. After all that had happened lately, he had to admit that it felt awfully good once he gave into it and let the smile come. "It is odd how folks tend to talk for hours about nothing and avoid the things that need to be said. If walking your rounds has taught me anything, it's that."

"I'm not sure how to take that, Clint."

"Just an observation. Actually, it's been a pleasure working for you, Sam."

"I'm the one that should thank you. But I'm not too sure

I like the sound of what you're saying. It sounds to me like you might already be thinking about moving on."

"Not just yet," Clint replied. "But let's get back to Anne's brother. Is there anything else you can tell me about Ken?"

The marshal craned his head back as though the answers he was after were written on the ceiling. After a few moments of consideration, he shook his head. "Not as such. I know he's been stationed at Fort Laramie for some time."

"Have you met him?"

"Actually, yeah. He's come here to visit his family a few times. I make it my business to check in with most everyone in town if I can and he seemed like a good sort. A little on the stiff side, but a good man."

"What do you mean by that?"

"Oh, nothing really. He just seemed like one of those military men who made those thick wool uniforms seem like a second skin."

"Ah, I think I've met a few of those men. The kind that can't let out a breath before lowering the colors and polishing their buttons."

Sam tapped the side of his nose and nodded. "You got that exactly right. I believe I saw him four or five times, now that I think about it, and not once was he out of his uniform or even slouching, for that matter."

Clint nodded and put those bits of information in along with all the others. Unfortunately, he was still a hell of a long way from getting a full picture.

"So do you think I should be more concerned about those fellas running around loose in my town?" Sam asked.

"They weren't exactly robbing that house just because it was empty," Clint answered. "And that means they were after something."

"From what you told me, that would be ol' Zack Michaels that they were after."

"That's right. And with your men guarding Zack and Anne both, we should have things covered. In the meantime, I'm going to see if I can try and figure out some more of this on my own. Something tells me that if I wait for it to resolve itself, we'll all be in for a rough ride."

Sam let out a breath and started pacing across the floor. "There's got to be something I can do to help. After all, that is what I get paid for."

"You can try and pull together some more men to act as a posse. Once I find out what's going on, we may need one."

"You got it. I know a few men that wouldn't mind signing on for some excitement. They're not exactly level-headed, but if push comes to shove, all we need is a few willing gun hands."

Clint didn't like thinking about it that way, but it was true enough. "One more question. Do you know anything about Fort Laramie?"

"Not really," Sam said offhandedly. "Just that they got plenty of soldiers stationed there and that they carry enough firepower to resupply plenty of the units that pass through these parts."

That dropped one hell of a piece into Clint's lap. Unfortunately, the picture he was starting to see wasn't too pretty.

TWENTY-FOUR

Blood.

Lots of blood.

That's about all Clint found when he went back into the home of the late Larry Brunell. He'd been hoping to find something that might help explain why all of that blood had been shed, but Clint wasn't so lucky. After his talk with Marshal Wise, he'd gone back to the house with a lantern in one hand and his Colt in the other. Even though Clint didn't expect to run into any more surprise visitors, he wasn't about to be caught flat-footed again.

It didn't take long for him to verify that there were indeed only two furnished rooms in the entire place. One of those was the small room where he'd found Zack tied to a chair, and the other was the bedroom facing out toward Anne's sewing room. Even in the bedroom, there was still blood spattered on the walls and floor, telling Clint that whatever struggle had taken place wasn't confined to one area.

Since there were tables and chairs knocked over here and there, Clint figured that a fight had started in the bedroom, and was over by the time Zack was brought into the room where he'd been tied up. Clint sifted through the room carefully, making sure to step only in places he'd already searched so as not to trample on anything important.

Apart from a bloody mess, Clint did find a few things that didn't seem to fit. They were cigar butts that had been chomped on and tossed onto the floor in the bedroom. By the looks of it, whoever had smoked them had spent a lot of time at the bedroom window. When Clint put himself in that same spot, he spotted a half-empty bottle of sarsaparilla sitting on the floor next to an overturned chair.

Clint picked up the bottle and examined it under the light of his lantern. There wasn't much he could tell about the stuff just by looking at it. He was no expert on that particular drink, but it smelled close enough to fresh as far as he could tell.

As much as he wanted to take a sip to see if the stuff was flat, the thought of drinking from the same bottle as some dirty killer didn't set too right with him. Instead, Clint placed his thumb against the top of the bottle and shook it up. When he took his thumb away, the sarsaparilla was bubbling well enough to answer his question.

That bottle couldn't have been sitting there too long, which meant that it had to have been brought in by someone there very recently. With the house's rightful owner stretched out on a table, that only left a few other contenders for the owner of that bottle. Nodding with satisfaction, Clint set down the lantern and went to work pulling the label off the bottle.

It was just a simple loop of paper with a few words printed on the front and came apart without much trouble. Clint folded the paper and put it in his pocket so he could read it somewhere where was more than a flicker of light. From there, Clint went on to check out the room where Zack had been tied up and tortured to within an inch of his life.

The smell of blood was still thick in the air, only now it was taking on a stale flavor. Once again, Clint was reminded of a slaughterhouse. Although there wasn't as much blood in that room as when fresh beef was stripped from the bone, there was an odd taint to the smell that told Clint he wasn't stepping in the remains of a cow.

Perhaps it was something instinctual, but there was something about human blood that set it apart. There was more of a rusty smell to it, or maybe it was a familiarity. Whatever it was, Clint wanted to do anything but stand around and think about it. At that moment, he just wanted to be anywhere but in that room.

Thankfully, there wasn't much else to see in that room apart from what he'd already seen. The chair and ropes were still there, right along with his and Anne's crimson footprints. Once Clint was satisfied with his second look, he left the room as well as whatever ghosts now resided there and headed straight for the stairs.

He stopped at the bottom of those stairs so he could stand quietly in that spot for a few moments. The lantern was turned down so he could just make out where he was walking without casting too many shadows. As he got closer to the door, he took those precautions to keep from announcing himself too loudly to anyone lurking nearby.

In those few quiet moments before leaving the house, Clint closed his eyes and listened to the creak of the boards as the wind blew outside. The house may have been just a collection of dead wood nailed together, but it was given a life of its own after being embraced by whoever had lived there. Once a house was completed, it got its own feel to it that was as distinct as the faces that passed through its doors.

Clint soaked up what he could feel, which told him for certain the place was empty. More than that, it felt as dead as its owner. When he left, he knew he'd never be coming back.

TWENTY-FIVE

There was one man standing outside Anne's house and before Clint could say a word to him, the fellow walked straight up to him.

"Don't worry, Mr. Adams," the younger man said, reading the obviously unhappy look on Clint's face. "The others headed to Doc Michaels' place. I'm staying behind to keep an eye on this place and let you know where they headed."

"Good, because I was all set to chew someone's hide for cutting Anne's guard down to one man so quickly."

"Yeah. I could tell."

"I guess it's been a long night. Where's Zack's place?"

The marshal's assistant gave Clint the directions he needed, and then started walking back to his post. "Don't worry none, Mr. Adams. I'll make sure nobody gets in here that don't belong."

Clint was fairly certain that if the men he'd been dealing with wanted to get by one kid with a pistol in his hand, they wouldn't have any trouble doing so. He was even more certain that those same men were more interested in the people living in those houses rather than anything else inside them. But rather than say any of that out loud, Clint gave the young man a friendly wave and went on his way.

Clint arrived at the little house situated a stone's throw from the town's business district. When he approached the three-room house, he immediately spotted the armed men posted next to and across from the front door. The guards nodded to Clint and let him enter.

"Thank God you're back," Anne said as she rushed forward to wrap her arms around him.

Clint gave her a hug and said, "You seem worse now than when everything was happening."

"I've had more time to think about it, that's all."

"Where's Zack?"

"In the next room. Jeremy's tending to him."

"How's he doing?"

"Zack or Jeremy?"

Shrugging, Clint said, "Start with one and go to the other."

"Zack's been restless, but he's hanging on. Jeremy's doing a fine job of cleaning him up and stitching up the bad wounds. Things have quieted down now, but the screaming was . . ." She drifted off for a moment to let a shudder pass through her. "It was pretty bad."

Clint had been around more than once when someone was getting treated after receiving a bad wound. He'd heard saws cutting through bone, and had heard more screams than he could stomach coming from strong men.

"Yeah," he said from experience. "I can imagine."

"I'm just glad you're back. I was starting to wonder if I was going to see you again."

Clint reached out to brush his hand along the side of her face. It seemed like ages since he'd made love to that same woman. In the time that had passed, enough had happened to fill most people's entire lives. "You need to get some rest, Anne. Why don't you lie down somewhere?"

"Perhaps I will. Now that you're back, I feel safe enough to close my eyes for a bit."

"You do that. I'll be in to check on you once I've had a talk with Jeremy."

The very prospect of going into the room where the younger doctor was sent another chill through Anne's skin. She didn't even pretend to want to go back into the room she pointed out to Clint. "He's in there," she said. "They both are."

"All right. Go on and I'll be with you shortly."

Anne nodded and walked into the next room. Every step took more effort than the one before it. Clint wondered if she wasn't going to fall asleep before even making it into the next room, but he saw her find a cot and lower herself onto it. Steeling himself, Clint faced the other room and walked through that door.

The first smell to hit him was once again the stench of blood. That scent was layered with others, however, such as the smell of alcohol and burning wood. The room was the biggest in the house, and had to be due to the stove that took up one corner. On that stove, water was being heated and used to douse towels that were wrapped around Zack's limbs.

Jeremy turned around to face Clint immediately. The younger man wore a troubled look on his face that made him seem to have aged twenty years since the last time Clint had laid eyes upon him.

"Oh, you're back," Jeremy said. "Hopefully you didn't find anyone else for me to treat."

"No," Clint responded, doing his best to look more comfortable than he felt. "Nothing like that. How's Zack coming along?"

Jeremy got up and shook his head while walking over to Clint's side. Dropping his voice to something barely louder than a whisper, he said, "He's hurt pretty bad, but he's hanging on. Between the wounds and the whiskey I've given him to ease the pain, he's fading in and out. He's out right now."

"Do you think he'll be able to talk soon?"

"What do you want him to say?"

"I need to find out anything he can tell me about who did this to him so I can track them down. Something big is going on here and I need all the help I can get."

Taking a breath, Jeremy blinked a few times as though he didn't know if he'd understood what Clint had just said. "Zack's lucky to be alive. I'm doing all I can to keep him that way. He's had a hand as well as parts of his feet chopped off, for God's sake, and you want to have him talk his way through it again? I'm sorry, but you'll just have to wait."

Clint put a hand on Jeremy's shoulder and squared himself off so that he was staring the younger man straight in the eyes. "I know he's hurt. I also know that no man would want to go through all of that and have the man that did it get away with it. He might have something important to say and if I don't try to hear it real soon, it may be too late."

Jeremy took a moment to absorb that. The anger that had been brewing in his eyes died down and he started to slowly nod. "You're right. It's just been a long night for me."

"You and me both, Doc."

"At least let him rest for a few more hours so he can catch his breath. He may be a little more coherent by then. He won't be feeling too good, but he'll be better than he is right now. Besides, you look like you could use some rest before you go chasing after anyone."

Clint's first reaction was to disagree, but the strain in every muscle of his body told him otherwise. "You've got yourself a deal. You mind if I use one of your cots?"

"Of course not."

"Is he back?"

The question was spoken in a haggard voice that sounded like it had barely come from the mouth of a human being.

Both Clint and Jeremy snapped their heads toward the voice, which had come from the opposite end of the room. Zack was struggling to sit up, and that prompted Jeremy to rush over and help him.

"You've got to sit still, Zack," Jeremy urged. "You'll break your—"

"Where's Clint?" Zack rasped. "I need to talk to him."

Before Jeremy could step in again, Clint was over at the wounded man's bedside. "I'm right here, Zack."

Zack forced the words out as though they'd been lodged in his throat. "They're in danger. All of them!"

TWENTY-SIX

Clint bent down closer to Zack's face so the wounded man didn't have to shout up at him. His first instinct was to comfort the man with a friendly pat on the hand or arm, but Clint pulled his own hand back before disturbing the fresh layers of bandages.

Meanwhile, Zack struggled to keep his eyes open and somewhat focused. He looked at Clint as though he was trying to talk to a dream that was already fading away. "Larry's dead," he croaked in breath that reeked of whiskey and blood. "They got him."

"I know," Clint said.

"But they didn't get the others."

"What others?"

"The ones . . . waiting for that stage. They meant to . . ."

When he saw Zack struggling even harder to form the words, Clint finished the sentence for him. "Those riders meant to kill everyone on that platform? Is that what you mean?"

Zack nodded even though the effort clearly wasn't too easy. "Meant to kill you too, but Larry most of all." The words came out of him in spurts. Sometimes, they were quick and lashed together, while other times they were slowly forced out from between pale lips.

Feeling an urgent tap on his shoulder, Clint looked to one side and found Jeremy there handing him a hot, wet towel. Clint took the towel and dabbed it over Zack's face. The heat seemed to calm the wounded man and his muscles relaxed. For a moment, Clint thought Zack might have passed out. But not only did Zack open his eyes again, they were a bit clearer this time around.

"You got me out of there," Zack said, acting as though he'd only just started speaking. "Thank you."

"Sorry I couldn't get there earlier."

"He was gonna kill me . . . just because I knew Larry so well. He and that other one . . . they laughed when they cut me. When I screamed, they just . . . stuffed sheets in my mouth and laughed and kept cutting."

Clint wanted to try to get Zack's mind off what had happened just to ease the man's spirit. He knew that would be impossible, however, and just tried to keep the words flowing. "Why did they do that to you? What did they want?"

"They . . . followed them . . . the people traveling together on that stage. Followed them ever since . . ." Zack started to struggle and clench his eyes shut. It wasn't so much because of pain, but because he just couldn't think of what he wanted to say next.

Suddenly, Clint felt as though the clouds had parted over his head. He reached for his pockets, frantically patting them down in search of something he knew was on him somewhere. Just when he was starting to wonder if he'd gotten rid of what he was looking for, his hand brushed against something in his inner jacket pocket.

Clint pulled the folded piece of paper out and straightened it so the wrinkled, dirtied surface could be read. "Here," he said, tapping to the date and location circled on the stagecoach schedule before the one he'd met up with on that platform. "Were they being followed since this stop right here?"

Zack squinted up at the paper. It took him a moment to read the times and locations printed there, but soon he started nodding furiously. "Yes, yes. That's it." He reached up to point to that first circled date while looking up at Clint. "Those men that got me were following those folks since this stop right here."

"Are you certain?"

"They mentioned that time and that town. I remember everything they said to me. Even though plenty of it didn't make sense, I'll never forget a word of it."

Seeing how intently Zack stared at the paper in his hand, Clint folded it neatly along its creases and put it back into his pocket. "Do you know why they were following them?"

Zack shook his head. Judging by the struggle in his movements and the way his eyes were glazing over, he was fighting tooth and nail just to stay conscious. "They asked me what Larry told me. What I knew. What he knew and what I knew about Martha, Krista, and Bill."

Hearing those names, Clint felt stupid for letting those people out of his sight. They were in serious danger and for all Clint knew, they could even be dead. But there was no way for him to know any of this until right now and there was no way of telling just how much longer Zack could hang on.

Putting his hand on Zack's shoulder and moving down a little closer to the man's face, Clint made sure he gave him something to focus on for just a little while longer. "Was there anything you were holding back from them?" Clint asked. "Anything at all? Or were they just torturing you because of some mistaken notion they had about what you knew?"

Zack looked up at Clint, and then moved his eyes so that he was looking beyond Clint's face. He seemed to be looking up at something only he could see when his eyes clenched shut and the pain seeped through them. "If I talked, I knew it would only cause more pain. But if I hadn't talked, I might not be dying right now. Lord help me, I just hope I did some good."

"What do you want to tell me, Zack?"

"It was something Larry told me. It was . . . something he was working on. Some kind of a deal. He was holding out to try and meet up with a man from the army. But it couldn't have been anyone local. It needed to be someone high up. Someone not from around here."

"Maybe someone from Fort Laramie?"

Zack's eyes widened as though Clint had just mentioned the name of the devil himself. "No! Those men . . . whatever they're doing . . . it's happening there. It's some kind of robbery."

"Like a payroll?"

"Money, guns, ammunition, everything. They're going to take it all." Now that he started talking, the information spilled out of Zack's mouth like a flood. "They got someone on the inside. Larry found out and was going to tell a reporter in Cheyenne. The others—"

"You need to rest, Zack," Jeremy said as he stepped up to the wounded man's bedside and placed his hand upon Zack's forehead. "You're burning up."

Clint held his ground even though he could see the color draining from Zack's skin. "Just a little more, Doc."

Jeremy moved in closer to his patient, and even went so far as to push Clint away from the bed. "His wounds are bleeding through the bandages. His fever is coming back and I need to end this right now!"

Allowing himself to be moved back, Clint kept his eyes on Zack. Not only was he certain that time was of the essence, he could tell that Zack knew it just as well. Clint hated to be callous to a dying man, but others would soon be joining him if something wasn't done.

"They're already there!" Zack shouted, his voice filling with desperate fire. "Men at . . . Laramie."

"Robbers?" Clint asked as he was shoved farther away. "Killers?"

Zack nodded, even as his body slumped down against his mattress and his energy dwindled. "In uniform. The others . . . saw the wolves. Just didn't . . . know it."

Jeremy gave Clint one last shove to push him out of the room. From there, he went back to his patient and hurried to do his best to keep Zack alive a few more minutes.

When Clint turned around, he was facing Anne. She looked at him and asked, "Wolves? Do you know what he was talking about?"

"Yeah," Clint replied. "He meant the kind in sheep's clothing."

TWENTY-SEVEN

Clint spent the rest of that night keeping himself very busy. Zack was a lost cause. As much as Clint wished it could be different, that was the simple truth. There was too much damage done to the man for it to be any different. In fact, Clint was surprised the man held on for as long as he did. Once Zack had said what he needed to say, that strength had been used up.

Wanting to make Zack's strength mean something, Clint rushed out of the doctor's office and made it his duty to find all the others that had been on that platform with him. With the help of Marshal Wise and a few other locals, Clint found out where those others were in less than an hour, and had even managed to gather them all in one place.

Sam came along with him and did a good job of keeping everyone calm despite the oddity of the situation and the intensity in Clint's eyes. That intensity didn't even start to fade until Clint could look around and see that all of the passengers had been reunited and that they were all safe. At least, they were safe for the moment.

"What's all this about?" Bill Grady asked. So far, of all the people gathered in the back rooms of the Wallace Social Club by Clint and Sam, Bill was the most vocal. Not

109

only was the short man barely half-dressed, but he was stomping around as though he was about to explode.

"I demand an explanation!" Bill stormed. "Jesus Christ, Sam, what the hell is going on?"

Marshal Wise stepped over to Bill and tried to put a friendly arm around the man's shoulder, but Bill shook it off immediately. "Take it easy, Bill," Sam said, ignoring the rudeness of his reception. "I was just getting to that." Looking around to the others gathered in the room, he said, "I'm sure some of you heard there was a ruckus earlier tonight involving Zack Michaels."

Krista and Bill nodded, but Martha didn't move a single gray hair upon her head.

"Well, there was some trouble over at the Brunell place and we don't want anyone else to get hurt."

Hearing this, most of those who had been brought to that room turned to look at Clint.

"What happened?" Krista asked.

Clint took a breath and let it out, partly to calm his nerves and partly because it felt as though he'd been on the move for about a week and a half. "The man we saw shot on the platform was Larry Brunell."

Although all of the people gathered in the room looked a bit confused, Bill was the first one to speak up.

"There was someone living in that place?" he asked.

"Yeah," Clint replied. "There was. Zack Michaels was a friend of his and something happened when he went over to check up on him."

"Oh, no," Martha gasped. "Is he all right?"

"No, ma'am," Clint said respectfully to the old woman. "He isn't."

That stirred everyone up and they began to nervously chat amongst themselves. Everyone, that is, except for Krista. She lowered her eyes and fell completely silent. Clint let them get some of the chatter out of their systems before pressing on with what he wanted to say.

"I had all of you brought here because I think there might be some danger to you. You should be all right so long as we keep an eye on you and you don't make it known where you are."

Bill let out a short, snorting laugh. "Is that why you dragged us all down here, to a whorehouse?"

Rolling her eyes a bit, Martha shot Bill a sideways glace as she grumbled, "I'll bet your face is better known around here than it is around your own dinner table, Bill Grady."

Holding back the laugh that the old lady had brought out in him, Clint kept a straight face and stepped in before Bill could fire back a reply. "For now, I just need you all to do as I say. Please. It'll make things easier all around. I promise you won't be here for very long. The lady who runs this place has agreed to put you up in nice rooms for as long as it takes."

"Lady?" Bill grunted. "You mean the madam? That was real neighborly of her."

Clint fixed his eyes on Bill's and responded without an ounce of the other man's sarcasm. "Yeah. It was."

Bill's face retained its crusty expression for a moment before he lowered his eyes and nodded.

"Anyhow," Clint continued, "you won't be here for long."

"How do you know that?" Krista asked. "What are you planning to do?"

"Let's just say that I'm not intending on letting what happened to Zack and Mister Brunell pass lightly."

"I would think that was the marshal's job," Bill pointed out.

"My job is to protect my town and its residents first," Sam said on his own behalf. "And that's exactly what I'll do. Too much blood has been spilled on my watch and I'll be damned if any more will follow."

Clint nodded and stood beside the marshal. "While he keeps you folks safe, I'll head out and see if I can get to the root of this whole matter. There's plenty going on and none of it is too good."

"What's going on, Mr. Adams?" Martha asked.

"Let's just say that you're better off not knowing more than you already do."

"That's funny. I feel like I don't know one bit of what's been happening around here."

"That's what I aim to clear up next. What I'd like to do is have a word with each of you in turn. I'll go over a few things and shed a bit of light here and there. You'll just have to trust me when I tell you that whatever I leave in the dark is for your own good."

Martha nodded and got up from her chair. "Well, a man earns my trust when he steps up the way you did back on that platform, Mr. Adams. And you haven't done anything but good for this town since you signed on with Sam. I'll be the first to talk to you. I just hope that I can help."

"Much obliged, Martha. I'll try to keep it quick and painless."

TWENTY-EIGHT

It was creeping up on dawn by the time Clint had had a chance to speak with all of the group he'd first met on that platform. One by one, he'd spoken to them to let them know the basics of what had gone on without telling them enough to put them in any more danger.

Knowledge was power and in this case, it was more of a powder keg that had already claimed at least one life. Clint winced as he thought about that. Better make that two lives. As he was talking to Bill, someone tapped on his door and informed him that Zack Michaels had died from the horrific injuries he'd been given.

Hearing that came as no surprise to Clint. In fact, he was more surprised that the doctor had made it as far as he did after the damage he'd endured. Unfortunately, if Clint was even half right about what was going on, there would be a whole lot more death on the way.

Krista was the last one Clint spoke to. She entered the room he'd been using and shut the door behind her. Clint had been careful to speak to the people separately to keep anyone from influencing another's story. He also wanted to get a look at their reactions when they were fresh and at their purest.

He didn't know for certain who he could trust, and being the only one in that person's sight made it even easier for Clint to catch any lies that were tossed his way. So far, the stories he'd been told had been simple and fairly consistent. There was always the possibility that they'd already gotten together to craft one big lie, but Clint doubted that.

Then again, that was also a possibility he really didn't want to consider.

"How far were you traveling?" Clint asked Krista after she'd sat down in one of the room's padded chairs.

"I was taking Cat home after visiting folks in Cheyenne. We'd gone other places as well, but that's where we started traveling by stage."

"How much farther did you travel?"

"Not much, I guess. Mostly on private properties owned by family."

"Anything strange happen when you first started riding the stage?"

"Not as such."

"Did you see anything that sticks out in your mind?"

Krista thought about it for a moment, and then let out an exasperated breath. "After that man was shot dead and with everything else that's happened, the rest just seems like a blur."

"What about any odd people you may have seen?" Clint offered as a way to jog her memory. "Maybe someone in uniform?"

Krista's eyes lit up and she nodded vigorously. "I do remember something like that! There was a fight! I remember seeing it when we were trying to catch the stage out of Cheyenne."

"Tell me about it."

"There wasn't much really. Two men came up on this other man in an army uniform. They started fighting, and soon another man in uniform came up to help, and before you know it, there were other men who came to start beating on him."

"Did you hear anything that was said?" Clint asked. "Anything at all as to why those men might be fighting?"

She thought about it for a good, long time, but eventually had to shake her head in defeat. "No. I'm sorry, Clint, but I just didn't. Once the fight started getting bad, I did my best to keep Cat from seeing too much of it so I missed out on a lot of it myself."

"That's understandable."

"I do remember that the fight seemed strange, though."

"How so?"

"I've seen a few fights before, and they always started out with someone being angry or yelling or something like that. This one didn't. It started off real quiet. I don't think anyone really noticed it was happening until it started getting messy."

This part wasn't unlike what had been said by all the others. Each of the passengers had gotten around to this same fight eventually. Although some of the details were remembered better than others, the basic story was always the same. Clint had picked up on that when fishing for anything to do with an army man or with Fort Laramie when he talked with Martha. Having picked up on that thread, he quickly found that it ran through everyone's account.

"How messy did it get exactly?" he asked.

Krista shuddered. "I didn't see it all, but I heard things getting pretty rough. At one point, the men in uniform were outnumbered. By that point, the fight moved into an alley, or somewhere out of sight. That was about the time when the stage was getting loaded, so that's about all I saw."

After taking a moment to let the memory go through her, Krista looked at Clint and asked, "Does that help?"

"Every bit helps. Was there anything else you could tell me about the trip? That is, before I came along."

She rattled off whatever details she could recall. Since she'd gotten past the previous block, there were quite a few details in her account, but none that went past the normal tedium of traveling from one town to another. Before she stopped, she even talked about when Larry was shot, and blushed when she reminded herself who she was talking to.

"I guess I can stop there," she said. "You know the rest. Ever since we've been back, things have been quiet. Then again, we haven't been back too long."

"I guess that does it then," Clint said.

"So does that mean you're still leaving?"

Clint nodded. "After I get some rest." As much as Clint wanted to get moving right away, he knew he wouldn't be much use if he collapsed from exhaustion when he was in the saddle or trying to deal with the killers he'd tangled with before.

Krista got up and walked to the door. She stopped with her fingers on the handle and turned to look at him over her shoulder. "You know something, Clint? This is the safest I've felt in a long time. You have that effect on people, you know?"

"I've never really been told that before. Sometimes, it seems to be the exact opposite."

"Well, it's true. Folks here feel safe with you acting on Sam's behalf. And I feel safe, even now. I wish I could make you feel that way." She walked closer to Clint and brushed her hands along his shoulders. "You feel so tense. I think I may be able to help you with that."

Reacting to the low, purring tone in her voice, as well as the touch of her hands on his knotted muscles, Clint was already feeling a whole lot better.

TWENTY-NINE

For a moment, Clint and Krista merely stood looking into each other's eyes. After all that had happened, Clint was feeling tired all the way down to the center of his bones. He could tell just by looking at her that Krista was feeling the same way. He could also tell that she was regaining her strength just as quickly as he was as they both let their hands rest on the other's bodies.

Krista's fingers drifted over Clint's chest, wandering down until they brushed against his belt. Clint had reached out to touch her as well. Before he realized what he was doing, the palms of his hands were grazing against her hips and moving upward along the smooth curves of her sides.

When his hands brushed against her breasts, Clint heard a lingering sigh escape from her lips. Their faces were so close together now that he could even feel the warmth of that sigh as her breath drifted past his lips. All Clint had to do from there was move forward less than an inch and his mouth was upon hers. When she felt him there, Krista wrapped her arms around him tightly and pressed herself against him.

At that moment, both of them were more than happy to let the rest of the world drift away. All that mattered just then was that neither of them wanted to stop kissing each other and that they had all the time in the world to indulge in one of life's simplest, greatest pleasures.

Clint had been thinking about riding through the night and sleeping somewhere along the way. He'd also been thinking about catching some sleep where he was and heading out before first light. Now, that decision had been taken out of his hands and he was perfectly happy with the outcome. Krista's body felt warm and receptive to every move he made. Her form seemed to melt against him, accepting him completely.

Pulling away slightly, Krista took a quick breath and snuck a glimpse toward the door. "What about the others?" she asked in a whisper. "Won't they wonder what we're doing?"

"Do you want to stop what we're doing?"

Closing her eyes and leaning back as Clint's hands slid down over her breasts and kept going until he cupped her buttocks, she replied, "No. God, no. Please don't stop."

"Then I say let them wonder." With that, Clint squeezed her tight little bottom in his hands and pulled her close enough to him so she could feel the erection growing between his legs.

Now, her hands were wandering lower over Clint's body, and they headed straight for his gun belt. Her eyes dropped down to watch as she unfastened the buckle. Clint was there to take hold of the holster and lower it to the floor, freeing her up to start removing his jeans.

As she peeled away his clothes, Krista felt her breath quickening and the blood racing through her veins. Her breath caught in her throat altogether when she felt Clint's hands sliding over her body and loosening the ties that held her dress tightly around her body.

Pulling the strings that laced up the sides of her bodice, Clint felt like he was unwrapping a present. Although the dress seemed like some kind of complicated mess of ties, hooks, and loopholes, pulling the right strings was enough to undo the whole lot. Her eyes darted up to his once the top of her dress came loose, and Clint looked right down at her to make sure she was still wanting to move on.

Although she seemed a bit bashful at first, there wasn't a hint of doubt on her face. In fact, her eyes flared a bit as Clint's fingers tightened around the top portion of her dress and slid it down so he could place his hands upon her breasts. The only thing between them now was the thin layer of cotton that was her simple white slip.

Krista had already unbuttoned Clint's shirt and now that they'd come this far, she pulled the shirt open so she could slide her hands beneath it and onto the muscles of his chest. Once she'd felt the warmth of his bare flesh, she ached to have his hands upon her naked skin as well, and wriggled impatiently as Clint pulled her slip down and over her hips.

After that, their hands moved on their own accord, removing every bit of clothing they could find until they were both naked in each other's arms. Clint held her around her waist, pulling her close as she reached up to lace her fingers together behind his neck.

From there, he walked her backward slowly until they got to the bed, which took up a good portion of the room. When Krista felt her calf bump against the bedframe, she lifted her leg to get onto the mattress. She stopped with her heel on the edge of the frame, however, as Clint's rigid penis pushed against the moist lips of her vagina.

They stood there for a moment, savoring the feel of each other, even enjoying the torture of being so close to penetration without allowing for that final push forward. The shaft of Clint's cock brushed against the wetness between her legs. As she shifted her hips gently back and forth, Krista could feel him getting even harder, and she started to moan softly at the thought of having him inside her.

Clint let his hands keep moving over her flesh, tracing

the generous lines of her breasts and allowing his thumbs to brush against her erect nipples. When his hands made it back down to the soft curve of her buttocks, Clint lowered her down onto the mattress and settled on top of her.

With her hands on his shoulders, Krista felt how the muscles in Clint's arms tensed as he leaned down to lower his face to kiss her. She spread her legs open reflexively when she felt his hips lowering as well. Krista's lips were pressed against Clint's, and when she felt the tip of his cock slip inside her, she opened her mouth and slipped her tongue into his.

Tasting her that way made Clint even harder, and he pushed his hips forward until he was completely inside her. Clint felt her gasp a bit as they kissed, and when he leaned back, Krista pushed her head back into the mattress and let out a soft, satisfied moan.

Clint looked down at her and watched as she arched her back when he pushed into her and didn't let out her breath until he was sliding out again. Sitting up a bit, Clint was able to put his hands upon her once more and massage her breasts as his hips took on a slow, pumping rhythm. Krista's body was impressive. Even when she was lying down, her breasts remained proud and full. Her rounded hips and buttocks fit perfectly in his hands. And her soft, red lips were unbelievably erotic as they parted to let out those breathy gasps.

When Krista opened her eyes again, she saw Clint moving between her legs. The sight made her even wetter, which allowed him to slide in and out at just the right speed. Without thinking about what she was doing, she reached up to take hold of one of Clint's hands and move it over her body.

Clint took her direction without hesitation, and found his fingers touching the sensitive nub of her clitoris while he moved in and out of her. Having her guide him like that excited them both, and when Clint started pumping faster,

Krista clenched her eyes shut, lay back, and enjoyed every second of it.

Soon, Clint wanted nothing more than to feel his body pressed against hers. When he lowered himself onto her so Krista's breasts were tight against his chest, she accommodated him perfectly, adjusting her body beneath him so he wasn't forced to break his powerful rhythm.

When she felt her climax approaching, Krista opened her legs wider and let him pound into her even harder. Clint could sense the tension building, and grabbed hold of the sheets so he could ride that tension all the way through to the end.

Their passion exploded at the same time, causing Clint and Krista to freeze at the moment of orgasm so the sensation of it could work its way through their entire bodies. When it passed, it left them weak and breathless. Clint rolled onto the bed and took Krista in his arms. They fell asleep that way with smiles on their faces, as though everything else in the world was just as peaceful as they felt.

THIRTY

Clint only managed to get a few hours of sleep, but he felt as rested as if he'd been in that bed for a day. He didn't much like the idea of leaving Krista there without so much as a word between them, but she looked so tranquil that he didn't want to take that away from her. Instead, he ran his fingers through her hair one last time, got dressed, and shut the door as quietly as he could when he left.

The first thing he saw once he was out of his room was the guard posted outside the room where he and Sam had talked to the others they'd collected. The guard noticed Clint immediately and gave him a nod.

"Is Sam still here?" Clint asked.

"He's around somewhere. Truth is, he hasn't sat still for more than a minute. He's been covering these halls, the streets, and any other place he can think of in between checking in on me and the others in here."

The young, burly man stopped for a moment to let a slender woman with long blond hair dressed in wisps of silk walk by. "Luckily, the only thing to see lately has been the ladies who work here."

Clint didn't mind seeing the young man's eye wander slightly at the sight of the working girl. If that was all he did, Clint figured the young man was holding up pretty damn well. Apparently, Duskin's whorehouse was run by real professionals. The madam kept business going without letting on that she was hiding a few stowaways in the process. The ruse wouldn't hold up forever, but Clint knew it didn't have to.

"Where are the others' rooms?" Clint asked.

Lowering his voice, the guard nodded to a few of the many doors as he pointed them out. "There, there, and there," he said. "The little girl's being watched by Miss Lilly herself."

Miss Lilly was the madam who was making this all possible, and Clint had dealt with her enough to know that she was a kind woman with a heart as big as her impressive bankroll.

Clint nodded. "All right then. If anyone asks for me, just tell them I'll be right back. Where was the last place Sam was headed?"

"To his post across the street. Look for the run-down building next to the newspaper office."

With that, Clint was heading down the hall toward the top of the stairs. Moving with stealth and speed, he was down the stairs and out the door without drawing any attention to himself. Considering the caliber of the girls Miss Lilly had working for her, the few customers in the place had plenty more to think about than one more man walking by.

When Clint stepped outside, he knew that he wouldn't be coming back anytime soon. He'd told the guard otherwise simply to make sure that nobody knew the complete story just in case the wrong people came snooping around. With the way things were stacking up, Clint didn't want to take any unnecessary chances.

It was early enough in the morning that the sun was still stuck behind a batch of stubborn clouds. That only gave extra teeth to the chill in the air and caused Clint to button his jacket all the way up around his neck. He spotted the building the guard had talked about immediately. In fact, Sam had used that same spot to watch the whorehouse one night when a bunch of rowdy cowboys had come into town. The marshal had been expecting trouble then, which paled in comparison to the trouble that eventually found its way into Duskin.

Clint didn't walk into that little shack until he was certain nobody was watching him. And when he opened that door, he made sure to do so nice and slowly. He stepped into the darkness with his hands in plain sight.

"You in here, Sam? It's just me."

"I see you there, Clint. Hell, I saw you the moment you stepped out of the social club."

"I hear you've been all over this town in the last couple of hours."

The marshal leaned forward from where he'd been sitting concealed in the shadows. "I figured I needed to keep my eye on everything around here before anyone else gets hurt. Speaking of moving around, where are you headed this early in the morning? Shouldn't you be getting some rest?"

"I did get some rest."

"Yeah, and I noticed Krista Myers was in there resting with you."

Although Clint could barely make out the other man's face in the near-total darkness, he didn't have any trouble picking up on the scowl that was surely there.

"She's getting some rest too," Clint said.

The marshal laughed under his breath, got up from his chair, and stretched his back. "I'll bet she needs it."

Both men paused for a moment before they allowed themselves to laugh off the comments Sam had been tossing in Clint's direction.

"You can really be an asshole sometimes. You know that, Sam?"

"Yeah, I know. I really do. Now how about telling me where you're headed. I know a man that's itching to get on the trail when I see one."

Clint nodded and glanced out the same window that Sam had been using to keep watch on the Wallace Social Club. "I'm riding out as soon as I'm done talking to you."

"Headed for Cheyenne or Fort Laramie?"

"First one and then the other." Clint didn't say anything more about the order, and hoped that Sam didn't ask.

"Yeah," the lawman said to the silence that followed Clint's answer. "I guess it's best none of us knows too much. Not after what happened to poor Zack."

"I'll wire you when I find out anything and I'll be back as soon as I can. You think you can handle things without me?"

"I've been a marshal long before the great Gunsmith came into this town," Sam growled. On a serious note, he added, "I'll be fine. I didn't have any trouble rounding up some men to lend me a hand after word got out about us losing Zack Michaels. Hell, I might even get some deputies out of this mess. Nothing's better than a crisis to get people to step up and lend a hand."

"Glad to hear it." Clint held his hand out to the marshal, which was quickly taken and shaken. "You know I hate leaving like this when there could still be—"

"Whoever's lurking around here have got a hell of a bad reception coming if they decide to stick their heads out. Just go and find out what lit this damn fuse. I'm dying to know myself."

"You got it, Sam. Take care of yourself."

Clint left through the shack's back door. From there, he went straight to the stables. Hopefully, Eclipse was ready to run.

THIRTY-ONE

The Darley Arabian stallion wasn't just ready to run. He practically chomped through the bit once Clint got the saddle and gear all in place. Once the horse knew he was going to be leaving the stable where he'd been kept for the last several days, he couldn't get moving fast enough.

Clint had ridden Eclipse into town when he'd first arrived to help out Marshal Wise. The ride had been long and before that, the stallion had been put through some rough weather on an even more strenuous ride. Because of all that, Clint figured the Darley Arabian had earned a rest. At least one of them could take it easy for a while.

Now that he was all rested up, Eclipse was a bundle of energy, and took off the instant he felt the flick of leather on his back. Clint had to hold on or be thrown off as the Darley Arabian built up to a fast trot and headed for the edge of town.

"What've they been feeding you while you were in there?" Clint asked as he gripped onto the reins and held on for dear life. "I'm glad one of us is feeling up to snuff."

Eclipse responded with a toss of his mane and a grumble in the back of his throat. Wanting to take advantage of the stallion's anxiousness, Clint snapped the reins as soon as they were out of town and allowed Eclipse to do what he'd been wanting to do since the moment Clint had walked into that stable.

The Darley Arabian's muscles moved like pistons beneath his skin and his head started churning back and forth as he built up momentum and speed. Riding in that saddle, Clint couldn't help but feel some of the horse's energy seep into him. That, combined with the rush of the wind and the drumming of hooves, made Clint feel as though he was ready to take on anything that got in his way.

Suddenly, it didn't matter what had happened before. It didn't matter that he still wasn't entirely sure what he was up against. All that did matter was the fact that he was charging forward and taking things back into his own hands. After all, with the head of steam they were building up, it was hard to imagine anything or anyone that could stop them.

Clint and Eclipse headed south with such speed that it felt like they'd sprouted wings. Before too long, Clint tugged on the reins until Eclipse's muzzle was pointed eastward as well, and he let the stallion run full out from there.

Just when he thought Eclipse was starting to tire out, the Darley Arabian would find yet another burst of energy that had been stored up while waiting in the stables. Clint too found his own reserves, and forgot about how tired he'd been feeling not too long ago.

It was times like these that reminded him why he'd never staked a claim somewhere or found a nice piece of property to start sinking some roots. The open trail was too deeply ingrained in him. He felt like he was only truly thriving when he was charging across the country with nobody to answer to except for the whims of fate.

It might have struck some folks as a peculiar notion, but it was true. The country may have been getting more crowded and there were fewer trails to blaze with every passing day, but that didn't mean it was time to stop looking.

For the moment, his eyes were fixed on the southeast horizon. The sun was burning through the clouds that had been fattening overhead until the rain that had been threatening to fall simply dried up. There was still a ways to go, but Clint's sights were already set on his destination.

Cheyenne was his first stop, even though Fort Laramie was much closer. Before he rode into the nest of vipers, Clint needed to find a way to spot the snakes that were hidden in the grass. Whatever the others had seen in Cheyenne had been important enough to kill over. Clint only hoped he could find out what he needed quickly before the snakes started slithering out of Fort Laramie's walls.

With that in mind, Clint gave the reins an extra snap and Eclipse was more than happy to oblige.

Even though the entire day was spent riding at nearly full gallop, it was one of the quickest days that Clint had ever spent. The hours seemed to flow by as quickly as the miles, and soon after the sun had dropped down past the western horizon, the town of Cheyenne was in Clint's sight. They approached the town like rolling thunder and when they came to a stop, Eclipse's chest was heaving like a pair of bellows.

As he swung down from the saddle to lead the Darley Arabian to the first stable he could find, Clint patted the horse's nose and scratched him behind the ears. "I know you were just getting used to the open trail, boy, but tonight you're sleeping in another stall. Don't worry, though. Neither one of us will be standing still for long."

THIRTY-TWO

By the time Clint got Eclipse a warm place to rest up and get fed, it was well past midnight. For a place like Cheyenne, however, that didn't mean the streets were even close to closing down. Some parts were quiet as a tomb, but just as many were only starting to wake up, and plenty of folks were walking or staggering from one door to another.

Clint could hear the music coming from several different saloons, as well as smell the liquor coming from the breath of several men who passed by. It was no wonder none of the people he'd talked to in the Wallace Social Club immediately recalled the fight that had happened. A place like Cheyenne was full to brimming with flying fists and smoking guns. A bigger trick would have been to go without seeing any scuffles for more than a few hours.

There were regular scuffles, and then there were scuffles that erupted into wars. Clint had seen enough fights to sniff out the ones that truly mattered, and he bet that the man he was about to see had that same kind of intuition. According to the letters painted on the front window, the building Clint approached held the offices of both the town and county law. He'd heard some things about Cheyenne lawmen, however, and he hoped that he might get some help despite those less-than-encouraging tales.

"Hello?" Clint said as he opened the front door and took a step inside. "Anyone here?"

The office was much larger than it appeared to be from the front. It was a narrow building that appeared to go all the way back to a number of cells in the rear. Several desks were scattered throughout the front room, only one of which was occupied at the moment.

Clint smiled at the tall, slender fellow sitting with his feet propped up on one of the smaller desks and gave a friendly wave. "Hello, there."

"Howdy," the man said with a curt, upward nod. "You here to check in?"

"Why, are there rooms to rent?"

The skinny man at the desk failed to catch any of the humor in Clint's reply, and instead got up so he could display the badge pinned to his chest and the gun hanging at his side. Hooking a thumb toward the cells, he said, "Plenty of rooms back there for smart-asses wasting my time in the middle of the night."

"Just a little joke," Clint said calmly. "It probably only seems funny to me because my brains are still rattling after riding all day long." After waiting for a moment to see that the lawman wasn't going to crack a smile at that one either, Clint got right to the point. "My name's—"

"You still haven't answered my question," the lawman cut in. "Are you here checking in?"

"Look, I just got here, so why don't you just tell me what you're talking about."

The lawman swung his feet down from the desk and stood up. He placed his hands at his sides close to his gun as a not-too-subtle warning. "That iron you're wearing. There's a new ordinance saying you need to check in with the law offices if you intend on bringing a firearm into town."

"Things been getting a bit rough?"

"You could say that. Town law keeps track of the guns, so that only leaves bottles and fists and such for the troublemakers to hurt each other with."

"How's that been working?"

The lawman shrugged. "It's a new ordinance. Still ironing out the wrinkles. Now how about that gun?"

Clint held his hands openly in front of him and slowly started reaching for the inner pocket of his jacket. "My name's Clint Adams. I've been working with the marshal of Duskin; a town about fifty miles or so—"

"I know where it is," the lawman said, his body visibly tensing as Clint's hand got closer to the inside of his jacket.

"I'm reaching for a paper that verifies what I say is true," Clint explained. Taking the edge of his jacket between thumb and forefinger, Clint opened it to show he wasn't wearing a shoulder holster. From there, he slowly removed the folded slip of paper that Marshal Wise had given to him to clear up any disputes as to his authority when working on the behalf of the law.

Although the local lawman's hand drifted closer to his weapon, he didn't draw it. Instead, he let Clint remove the paper and hand it forward. After taking the paper and glancing over it, the fellow relaxed a bit and nodded. "Looks official."

"Does that mean I'm properly checked in?"

"Yeah. Normally, I like to have a stranger leave his guns with me, but I guess I can make an exception. Ed's been signing on some new folks up there in Duskin."

"You mean Sam, don't you?"

Now, the lawman's body relaxed even more and a sly grin crossed onto his face. "Yeah, I do. Sam doesn't sign his name on these here slips, which is a way to catch forgeries and such. You'd be surprised how many bad men try to fly the colors of the law to justify their killing."

"Actually, I wouldn't be too surprised. Cheyenne can be a rough town."

The lawman handed the paper back to Clint and leaned against his desk. "Clint Adams, huh? You wouldn't be The Gunsmith, by any chance, now would you?"

"Actually, I would."

The lawman nodded and started picking something from between his teeth. "Yeah, Sam wired me earlier today and said you might be stopping by."

When he saw the confusion start to show upon Clint's face, the lawman let out a chuckle and reached out to slap Clint on the shoulder. "Sam and I go way back, but you can never be too careful. The name's Allan Reader. Sam might have told you about me. I'm the one that gave him a hot-foot last time he came here to deliver a prisoner."

Clint was torn between thinking the lawman was crazy and thinking he'd just gone for too long sitting at his desk instead of getting some much-needed sleep. "Uh, no. Sam never mentioned that."

"Well, we joke around all the time. Breaks up the tension. Sam and I have been going back and forth for years. I pull one over on him and he makes like he wants to knock a chair over my head. It's just good fun."

The smile on the lawman's face was genuine enough, but didn't make it any easier for Clint to decide whether or not he was a sandwich or two shy of a picnic.

"So, all this business with checking in . . ." Clint said tentatively.

"Was the way I'd treat anyone I never seen before. Like you said, Cheyenne can be a rough town. Especially nowadays. Besides," the lawman added with a broadening smile, "I thought I'd give you a bit of a hard time just to let you know any friend of Sam is a friend of mine. Welcome to Cheyenne, Clint."

Reaching forward to shake the hand the lawman offered, Clint saw the fellow's hand twitch toward his gun.

The lawman laughed when he saw Clint's eyes narrow, and then shook his hand for real.

After a hard day's ride and all that had been going on, Clint wasn't in the mood for joking around, especially when it involved pretending to draw a gun on him.

Tough town indeed.

THIRTY-THREE

Allan Reader was the town law in Cheyenne. Actually, he was one of several men acting as town law who worked out of the same office as the county lawmen. The office itself was mostly a formality since Cheyenne kept the lawmen busy enough to spend the vast majority of their time walking the streets.

Clint didn't bother bringing himself up to date on getting the names of the lawmen in charge because he hoped to get what he needed from the man in front of him at the moment. Reader was a slender man who appeared bony when he actually got up and started moving around. His cheeks were sunken and covered with dark bristles. His nose hooked down and flared whenever he inhaled.

After spending just a minute or two with Reader, Clint was even more anxious to move on than when he'd stormed into town. Still, the lawman seemed eager to help.

"Sam and I go a ways back," Reader said, making himself comfortable behind his desk and motioning for Clint to do the same in one of the nearby chairs. "Of course, it's been a while since I heard from him. Now when I hear that he's got a problem and Clint Adams himself may be coming to Cheyenne on his behalf, that's damn impressive."

"Yeah, about that—"

"We hear your name a bit around here, in the saloons and such. Of the ones that say it, half of the men claim to be you and the other half claim to have killed you."

Trying not to show how much frustration was building up, Clint forced a smile onto his face and said, "That happens sometimes. Now, what I wanted to ask you was—"

"I'll bet if we go into any saloon down the street, I can find a half dozen men who'll say you're not even—"

"Excuse me, Allan," Clint interrupted, using the most polite tone he could manage, "but as much as I'd like to shoot the breeze, there is some important business I need to discuss."

That seemed to snap Reader out of his musings. At least, it did for the time being. "Yeah, yeah. Right. Sorry about that. What was it that's so important to bring you all the way to Cheyenne?"

"There have been some shootings."

"We get plenty of those around here."

"They don't get so many of them in Duskin and these seem to be connected to something bigger than a saloon fight."

"Really? How big are we talking here?"

"Big enough that the last man who knew much about it was tortured so badly that there wasn't a doctor in the world that could save him."

"Jesus. What can I do to help?"

"I needed to ask you about a fight that happened here not too long ago." Clint went on to tell Reader about the scuffle that had been described by the witnesses who'd seen it. He told the lawman as much as he could regarding when and where the fight had happened as well as whatever he knew regarding a description of the combatants. He also slipped in a description of the men he'd fought in Zack's house. When he did that, Clint realized just how little he'd seen of one of those men.

All the while, Reader listened and nodded. Finally, he snapped his fingers and said, "You know what? I do remember hearing about a fight between some army boys down where those stages get loaded. And I believe it happened right around when you were saying."

"How much do you recall?"

"Well, I wasn't there myself. Actually, none of us were. The only way we heard about it was when the body was found."

Clint felt something in his stomach that was a mix of excitement and dread. "What body?" he asked.

"The body left behind by that fight."

As far as Clint had heard, the fight had been bloody, but not exactly fatal. Rather than go into that with Reader, he simply nodded and said, "Go on."

"We get plenty of folks tossing punches around here, and even with as much law as we got in this town, there ain't enough time in the day to go around busting up every brawl. We got word that some men in uniform were mixing it up down by the stagecoach station, and since we don't want any innocents getting hurt, some deputies were sent down to have a look.

"Anyhow, they come back and said there wasn't no fight. Just to be sure, the county sheriff sent them back to have a better look, and that was when the body was found."

"Whose body was it?" Clint asked.

"It was the damnedest thing. I do recall hearing, and this is what made it stick out in my head, that the body was stripped right down to his long underwear, but his gun wasn't too far from him. He was missing his watch and every other kind of valuable, but a perfectly good firearm was left right there."

"The body," Clint repeated. "Whose was it?"

"Whoever it was, sure as hell was robbed by a damn idiot. Those pistols are worth more than whatever he had in his pockets, that's for—"

"I was looking more for a name," Clint said, feeling his patience straining like a string that was close to snapping. "Do you know the dead man's name?"

Reader's eyes scrunched up and he gnawed his top lip for a moment before giving up and pulling open a drawer in the neighboring desk. "I think he's still got it wrote down here," he grumbled, flipping through some papers in the other desk. Finally, he nodded and pointed to one particular sheet he'd found. "Here it is. The boy's name was Mortenson. Kenneth Mortenson. I guess someone nearby recognized him."

Somehow, hearing that name wasn't much of a surprise to Clint. Although he'd been expecting Anne's brother to be caught up in this, he'd been expecting to find the master sergeant alive rather than dead and stripped in an alley.

"What about the gun?" Clint asked.

Reader got the gun for him and handed it over. It was a standard-issue army model Colt revolver, and a quick once-over told Clint that the gun hadn't been fired.

"Is this just how it was found?"

Reader nodded. "Yep. County law's a stickler for keeping things just right."

That may have been true, but there was nothing right about the picture that was coming into focus. Nothing right at all.

THIRTY-FOUR

Clint was allowed to go through all the reports written about the fight he'd been asking about. Of course, those reports consisted of not much more than a few lines scribbled into a ledger that told him about a quarter of what he already knew. Considering what he'd learned already, however, his trip to Cheyenne was far from useless.

"Will any of the others be able to tell me anything else?" Clint asked. "Maybe a deputy or whoever found the body?"

Reader shrugged. "Maybe. Maybe not. What else were you looking for?"

Clint thought about the answer to that question, and came up with an answer that was much easier than trying to track down another lawman and get him to talk. "How many hotels are in town?"

The lawman shook his head quickly as if the change of topics had physically rattled him. "Quite a few. Why?"

"Too many for us to visit in one night?"

"Probably not, but why would you want to do that?"

"I don't suppose you could tell me the names of any other army men to come through Cheyenne recently?"

"Not hardly."

"And do you think any of the other lawmen in town would know?" Clint asked.

"Probably not."

"But I'm betting that they signed a register somewhere in town when they rented their rooms."

"Yeah. Could be they stayed with friends or family too."

This time, it was Clint who shrugged. "And looking for names in those spots would be like digging for a needle in a haystack, so let's go with checking out the registers. I'll also need you to tell me which saloons have rooms to rent as well. This isn't my first time in Cheyenne. I'm pretty sure we should be able to cover most of the places in a few hours."

"Aw, Jesus," Reader said, rolling his eyes.

"What's the matter? You have better things to do?"

"No, but someone's supposed to stay in the office at all times in case there's . . . well, if there's a need for . . . aww, hell." Reader snatched his coat from where it was resting on the back of his chair. He then got his hat and slapped it on top of his head. "Let's get moving. If Sam wants me to help you, then I'd best do it. Besides, I could use the chance to stretch my legs."

As daunting as the task seemed, it wasn't so bad once Clint and Reader just set their minds to it and got moving. Compared to his conversation with Reader, Clint found the hotel workers and saloon owners to be several times more accommodating. They had businesses to run and no time to waste. That made for some short, no-nonsense talks.

If Reader was good for anything, it was taking Clint to the best spots the uniformed men liked to frequent, whether that meant saloons, brothels, or hotels. In less time than he'd expected, Clint was getting some of the names that he wanted.

While none of the names struck him as familiar, Clint wrote them down all the same along with whatever other information he could get. Where the hotel owners were good for recalling faces and dress, the saloon owners were good for recalling who looked like trouble and who'd been in town before.

After a few hours, Clint and Reader were feeling about the same. Their legs were tired from all the walking and their throats were sore from all the talking. On the other hand, Clint's list had been narrowed down to a manageable level, and he'd even gotten more than enough notes to put some details to the unfamiliar names.

The sky was turning a light purple as dawn approached like some kind of surprise attack. When Clint and Reader looked up into the sky, they squinted as though they hadn't been expecting to see anything but the same old stars.

"Is it that late already?" Reader asked.

Clint checked his pocket watch and nodded. "Early is more like it. You think your deputies are starting to wonder where you are?"

"Eh, I doubt most of 'em are even done cleaning up some of the messes they get into."

"The places we visited didn't seem too rowdy."

"You don't know these lawmen like I do. Some of the messes they deal with aren't exactly out in the open." Lowering his voice and nudging Clint with an elbow, Reader added, "And some of 'em didn't even start until the deputies got there, if you catch my meaning."

Clint had no trouble catching that meaning. In fact, it was a meaning that held true for plenty of the bigger towns. Places like Cheyenne and Dodge didn't get saddled with a reputation for no good reason. They earned those reputations, and plenty of lawmen got rich off of keeping those reputations firmly in place.

"Well, I'll let you get back to your office or wherever you need to go," Clint said. "I appreciate you taking time out to show me around. It helps having a familiar face next to you when you're trying to get folks to talk."

"Not a problem, Clint. Just be sure to send my best to Sam when you get back. And give him a hotfoot for me before you leave Duskin. He'll get a hoot out of that!"

"I'll bet he will. Thanks again."

With that, Clint parted ways with Reader and headed in the opposite direction. Rather than saddle up and leave right away, Clint went to one of the hotels that had been the quietest of the bunch he'd visited. It also seemed farthest away from anything remotely associated with the mess Clint was dealing with.

It was good to rest his eyes, if only for a few hours, in someplace quiet. Those types of places were few and far between in Cheyenne. After not much more than a three-hour nap, Clint was back in the saddle and riding northwest toward Fort Laramie.

As far as he was concerned, it was the eye of the storm.

THIRTY-FIVE

Eclipse was more than willing to charge all out toward Fort Laramie. Spirit was never a problem with the Darley Arabian, but Clint was more concerned about the horse's body. Riding too hard for too long was a good way to break the strongest of animals, and Clint wasn't about to do such a thing to Eclipse.

They covered plenty of ground at a medium pace. Every so often, Clint would allow the stallion to run, but would rein him in when he felt the muscles straining too hard beneath Eclipse's flesh. It wasn't anything Clint could pinpoint, but more of an instinct he'd gotten after traveling across this and a few other regions on that horse's back.

There was a certain bond formed between a man and his horse that was a cross between being partners, friends, and caregivers. Sometimes, Clint was hard-pressed to say who was caring for who, since he would have been dead several times over if not for Eclipse coming through when he was needed.

It was for the sake of that bond that Clint resisted the urge to forsake everything else just to get to Fort Laramie as quickly as possible. That wasn't to say that he took an easy day's ride, but Clint didn't feel the wind in his face quite as strongly as when he'd ridden into Cheyenne. Eclipse was grateful for the run, but was equally grateful to get the occasional rest. Clint could tell that much by the way the stallion reacted when the reins were pulled and they picked a spot to graze and catch their breath.

Clint took these moments to sort out what he'd learned so far. First of all, he knew that people were being killed for having seen or heard something they weren't supposed to. Where he'd thought that Larry Brunell had been the only intended target, it now looked as if Zack was right and everyone on that platform was meant to die in that first attack.

Clint himself might very well have been a target since the men he'd encountered in Larry's house seemed to know exactly who he was. That thought didn't get much more than a passing bit of notice from Clint. After all, he was used to getting such cold receptions.

The second thing he'd learned was that Fort Laramie was the target of the plan that was being carried out. Clint doubted it was just a robbery, but even if it was, there was bound to be plenty more bloodshed in the process.

Third, Clint had discovered a few names of soldiers that had been in Cheyenne when Anne's brother Kenny was killed. Clint cringed at the thought of telling Anne that her brother was dead, since she didn't seem to have the faintest notion. That hadn't set well with him all day long, but not just because he didn't like being the bearer of bad news.

If Ken Mortenson was a master sergeant, how could he have been killed several days ago without his family being informed? Lines of communication weren't always fast-moving, but with Duskin being less than a day's ride away, Anne should have known about it by now. That meant either she was lying, or Ken's death was being covered up for some reason.

Clint had looked into her eyes when Anne talked about her brother, and hadn't detected anything that made him think she was trying to pull something over on him. While he didn't think his judgment was ironclad, Clint trusted it enough to think there was something else he had yet to discover.

Walking a few feet from where Eclipse was wandering and eating whatever scraps of grass he could find, Clint dug the paper out of his pocket that he'd used to write a list while touring Cheyenne with Reader. The list was made up of names, ranks, and physical descriptions that Clint had gathered from all the locals he'd met. It was rare that each person on the list had all three bits of information noted, but Clint had enough jotted down to make him feel like he'd accomplished something.

He could hear Eclipse making some restless noises nearby, and when Clint looked over there, he saw the stallion was raring to go. Eclipse paced anxiously and bobbed his head when he saw Clint was glancing his way. All Clint had to do was start moving in that direction, and Eclipse walked the rest of the way toward him.

"I know how you feel," Clint said as he climbed into the saddle. "After all this talk about Fort Laramie, I'm pretty anxious to get there myself."

As he snapped the reins, Clint went over it all again, starting with the account Zack Michaels had given him. All of those thoughts flew from his head, however, when Clint spotted the flash of black and white in the distance. It was a ways off, but there was no mistaking that Appaloosa since Clint felt as if he'd been chasing it for weeks.

THIRTY-SIX

Despite the considerable distance between them, Clint could tell the moment the rider of that Appaloosa knew he'd been spotted. It was as if that moment stuck in time for a little bit, allowing both men to meet the other's gaze and hold it. It wasn't an altogether unfamiliar feeling for Clint. He'd felt it several times when he was either the hunter or the hunted.

When the moment passed, the Appaloosa turned around and bolted away. Clint responded in kind by snapping the reins and touching his heels to Eclipse's sides just to get that extra burst of speed right at the get-go. The Darley Arabian let out a whinny, and was off like he'd been shot from a cannon.

Keeping that Appaloosa in his line of sight, Clint wasn't about to ignore everything else around him. The terrain was flat and whatever trees were around were still mostly bare from dropping their leaves to the ground. There were still plenty of places for an ambush to be sprung, especially with Clint riding almost as fast as the wind itself.

From what he could tell, the other rider was heading roughly toward Fort Laramie as well. There were a few deviations from that course thrown in, but the general heading remained the same. Clint was careful not to follow perfectly because if he was being led into a trap, he could be riding into any number of them and wouldn't know until one of them had been sprung.

The sound of the Appaloosa's hooves beating against the earth mixed with the rumble of Eclipse's to form a kind of rolling thunder that enveloped Clint on all sides. A pounding echo was left behind in their wake, and it seemed to take several seconds before the ground stopped shaking.

As he rode and watched the area around him, Clint had to admit that the Appaloosa was one hell of an impressive animal. Even with Eclipse going at a full gallop, the other horse was still occasionally pulling ahead. But when that animal would slow to catch its breath, Eclipse would start closing the gap just enough to keep the other from getting away.

Clint waited to pour on whatever reserves Eclipse had left for just the right moment. He knew the Darley Arabian could add just a bit more power to its strides, but that kind of speed wouldn't last long before doing some damage. Clint knew he would feel when the time was right for that extra burst.

Not just yet, but the time was getting close.

Not yet.

The moment loomed closer and closer like an orchestra building up to its crescendo.

Finally, as Clint found himself leaning even more forward in the saddle, he let out a breath that was part command and part war cry. With the sound that came from the back of his throat, he snapped the reins and held on for dear life.

The Appaloosa appeared to have matched Eclipse's speed for a moment, but only for a moment. After that, Clint could tell he was getting closer to the other horse. It was closer than he'd been since this chase had started, and just as he fixed his eyes on the rider, who grew larger with each passing second, he forced himself to look away.

They'd been hiding behind a cluster of tree stumps along the route the Appaloosa had taken. Clint was just about to pass them when he spotted a flicker of movement coming from behind one of the solid wooden forms.

It had been a trap. Once again, Clint had to give the other rider credit for nearly springing that trap successfully even though Clint himself had been fully expecting to find one. Even after he saw the other men stand up and lift rifles to their shoulders, the notion of continuing after the Appaloosa still went through his mind.

It was tempting, since that was the man he'd been after from the very beginning and he was so close to running him down. Then again, no matter how fast Eclipse could move, each one of those rifles could spit out lead that moved a hell of a lot faster.

Pulling back on the reins, Clint wanted to let out a yell that could have been heard by the man pulling away on the Appaloosa in front of him. It came from the frustration of having to let him get away yet again after all that he'd done. Clint wasn't in the habit of allowing men to get away with taking shots at him, but that was exactly what he did when he steered Eclipse off to one side.

Even as he turned away from his prey, Clint could still see that black and white spotted hide getting further away. Letting him go at that moment was like folding after being dealt four aces. Still, he would have felt something a whole lot worse if he allowed those riflemen that had stood up to get a clear shot at him or Eclipse.

As if answering that thought, the first shot cracked through the air. If he hadn't pulled into such a sharp turn, Clint would have felt that bullet dig right through his rib cage. That shot was followed by a few more as all the riflemen pulled their triggers.

Now that he'd completed the turn and was headed back in the opposite direction, Clint got a look at the firing squad that had been waiting for him to race by. There were four of them in all, two hiding behind each cluster of old stumps. Judging by the gnawing in his stomach, Clint sensed that the next round of gunfire was set to go off at any moment.

He responded to that instinctively by lowering himself down until he was almost lying flush with Eclipse's neck. That way, Clint could steer by leaning his body one way or the other while also giving the riflemen a much smaller target. It wasn't the easiest way to ride and Eclipse wasn't exactly used to it, but it kept Clint from getting picked out of the saddle by the lead that hissed through the air over his head.

Every second or so, Clint would shift Eclipse's course before the riflemen could adjust to the last one. The irregular zigzag motion kept either of them from getting hit, but that came as a small consolation. He knew the Appaloosa was already long gone.

THIRTY-SEVEN

The Appaloosa moved like a machine beneath Ed Novak's saddle. Its muscles churned like pistons and mighty lungs filled and emptied with strength and precision. When he was in the saddle, Ed felt as though he could fly, and when his hand closed around his gun, he felt as though he wore the black shroud of death itself.

Having Clint Adams try to catch him was like running at the front of a tidal wave. If his pace faltered in the slightest, Ed knew his life itself could come screaming to a halt. But that would never happen. Not so long as he kept his horse running and his brain running even faster.

The ambush had been a product of Ed's brain and he knew, no matter how much anyone else told him different, that Adams would charge straight into it. He could feel the connection between himself and Adams as though they already had their hands wrapped around each other's necks. Ed grinned when he thought of that particular image.

"Soon," he whispered while bringing his horse to a stop and turning to get a look at the ambush. "Real soon."

The fight was happening a ways off, but Ed could see plenty of it from where he was. Shots cracked through the air, the sounds of which were only rattling echoes by the time they reached Ed's ears. He could see the puffs of smoke, and the occasional spark as well, which made him want to enter the fray before it was over.

Then again, by the looks of things, it was going to be over in less time than it would take for him to get there. Ed could also see that if things kept heading the way they were, he would still have his chance to test Adams's mettle.

Ed admired the horse Clint rode at that moment more than the man himself. That Darley Arabian practically danced around the bullets being thrown at him, making crazy turns and tossing his head about like some kind of raging storm.

The sight was something to behold, and Ed could have sat there watching it all day. In fact, he'd even admired the thunder of that animal's hooves as it had nearly chased him down. In fact, without the ambush that had been sprung, Ed thought that Darley Arabian might have had a shot of catching him.

But that seemed like blasphemy, and Ed regretted it the moment that thought crossed his mind. Even though the Appaloosa had no way of knowing what Ed was thinking, the man felt compelled to reach out and pat the horse apologetically.

"Don't you worry none," he whispered into the animal's ear. "This could be over any second."

But Ed didn't even believe that for as long as it took him to form the words. He watched as Clint and that horse rode circles around the riflemen that had been covering Ed's back. He also watched as Clint leaned from one side of that Darley Arabian to the other, squeezing off shots that knocked the riflemen back and eventually off their feet.

Rather than stand there any longer, Ed brought his horse around and flicked the reins. Watching any more would have defeated the purpose of the ambush altogether, and the sacrifice of those men would have been in vain. Of course, the riflemen hadn't known they were being sacrificed like that, but that was beside the point.

What mattered was that Ed got away from there and to Fort Laramie before Adams. There was too much at stake to start taking bigger risks now. Compared to what was brewing, even going up against The Gunsmith himself was small potatoes.

As much as he wanted to watch how Adams worked, Ed got moving away from the ambush site. In no time at all, the Appaloosa was tearing across the ground like some kind of elemental force. A smile drifted onto Ed's face as he leaned forward and felt the wind flow over his back.

There was no way Adams could catch him now.

No matter how close he'd gotten in the past or how impressive that Darley Arabian truly was, there was simply no way in hell for Adams to catch up after the head start Ed had made for himself. A victory like that might have been small in the scheme of things, but it was monumental in Ed's mind.

Now, not only would he be one of the richest men in the country, even a man responsible for numerous shifts in power, but he would be the man who'd truly beaten Clint Adams at his own game. Ed had outthought, outmaneuvered, and outrun The Gunsmith.

All that was left was for him to outshoot the legend known as Clint Adams, and that was coming up real soon.

THIRTY-EIGHT

It seemed as though the entire world was swirling around Clint's head. Eclipse's hooves pounded the earth and his body was leaning to one side so much that it was only his momentum that kept him from falling over. In fact, it was Clint that was doing all the circling, and he wasn't the only one being made dizzy by the constant motion.

The riflemen who'd sprung the ambush kept trying to take shots at Clint, but couldn't hit their target because they couldn't quite gauge what Clint's next move would be.

For a horse his size, Eclipse was turning quickly and without warning. One moment he was charging to the right, and in the next moment, he was bounding to the left. As his head turned one way, his body would suddenly swerve the other. Even Clint was impressed with how well Eclipse responded to every erratic instruction he was given through a combination of the reins and Clint's arms and legs.

It was a moment of pure poetry, and it would have been a whole lot easier for Clint to enjoy if there hadn't been men shooting at him every step of the way. But the shooting stopped soon enough. While Clint was zigging and zagging, he was firing off rounds from his Colt as well.

And when he'd pulled his trigger the last time, he finally brought Eclipse to a stop.

The stallion's chest heaved in powerful gusts, and Clint felt a film of sweat on Eclipse's coat as he dropped down from the saddle to land upon the ground. Knowing the horse would only need a few moments to recover, Clint turned his attention to more pressing matters.

"You," he said to one of the riflemen who was still moving. "Start talking."

The other man was lying on the ground with his rifle lying not too far away. He was still blinking his eyes and looking in all directions as though Clint was still circling crazily around him. When he tried to reach for his gun, he winced in pain. It was only then, it seemed, that he realized he'd been shot through both shoulders.

Just to be certain, Clint walked over to the rifle and kicked it away. He stood there and looked off in the direction that he'd last seen that elusive Appaloosa run to. He didn't think he'd see a trace of that horse after letting it slip away. Unfortunately, Clint was right.

"I've got things to do and places to be," Clint said. "But if you make my job easier, I'll do my best to make things easier for you."

"Like how?" the rifleman grunted. "By finishing me off with a bullet to the head?"

"That's a bit dramatic. I was actually thinking more along the lines of taking you with me instead of letting you struggle to the nearest doctor with only those two fresh wounds for company."

The rifleman blinked a few times and took a deep breath. Pain worked its way through his body like a set of slow, raking claws. He knew his wounds weren't exactly fatal, but he wouldn't be able to patch them up too well on his own. Whatever second thoughts he'd been entertaining quickly vanished once he got a look at the bodies of the others who'd been a part of the ambush.

"What do you want to know?"

Clint nodded and holstered the Colt. "Now you're starting to come around," he said while tearing strips from the rifleman's shirt to use as makeshift bandages. "First, I need to know what's going on at Fort Laramie."

Pulling away and wincing at the pain that motion caused, the rifleman said, "Then you might as well kill me. If it gets back that I said anything, I'm as good as dead."

Actually, Clint had only asked that question to make sure that the rifleman had been sent from Fort Laramie and that the same place was still the eye of the storm. The man's response had been more than enough to clear that up for good.

"Fair enough," Clint said, shrugging as though he was truly conceding something. "Then how about telling me how many men are at the fort that I need to worry about?"

Clint had played enough poker to recognize when a man was considering folding. Although the rifleman was close to the breaking point, he wasn't moving fast enough. Clint may have been cool and collected on the outside, but on the inside he was aching to get back in the saddle and on his way.

"It's a small price to pay for a ride to somewhere you can get those wounds stitched up properly," Clint said, tying the material around the wounds so the man would at least make it before bleeding out. "Especially when you consider the fact that I'll make sure to run your horses off from wherever you fellas stashed them."

That turned the rifleman's eyes wide as saucers, and Clint nodded again to let him know that he was indeed serious.

"Besides," Clint added as a way to speed things up, "it's not like I won't find out for myself soon enough once I get there."

That was all the rifleman needed to hear. "Fine, fine. About half the soldiers stationed there are sided with Novak. I don't know for certain exactly how many, but it's a lot."

"And what about the ones giving orders?" Clint asked. When he saw the questioning look in the rifleman's eyes, he said, "I know about them. How many are there right now?"

Letting out a breath that was pained by more than just the bullet wounds, the rifleman replied, "Four. At least, that's how many were there the last time I was."

"There now. That wasn't so hard was it?"

The rifleman didn't say another word. He didn't need to. He'd already said more than enough and both he and Clint knew it.

After dressing the wounds as best he could without wasting more valuable time, Clint got them both back on the way to Fort Laramie. It didn't take much time to get the location of the horses from the rifleman and even less time to get the wounded man saddled up.

"Wait a minute!" the rifleman said when he saw Clint turn Eclipse away and start riding. "You're just leaving me here? I can barely ride. I think I'm starting to see double!"

"I'll send a doctor for you."

"But I don't think I can wait long."

"Don't worry about that," Clint replied before snapping the reins. "You won't have to."

THIRTY-NINE

Clint hadn't been lying when he told the wounded rifleman that he wouldn't be waiting long for help. As close as he was to Fort Laramie and all that waited for him there, Clint had every intention of riding hard until he got there. He'd seen plenty of wounds, and knew a man could survive with the ones that rifleman had for a while before things got too serious.

Besides, Clint reminded himself, that man had put his own life on the line when he'd taken up his rifle and pulled the trigger.

That was about the extent of the sympathy Clint could dredge up for the rifleman. Considering how close all of the ambushers had gotten to knocking Clint from the saddle, he thought he was being awfully charitable. From there, he turned his attention toward the trail he was riding.

That trail ended at Fort Laramie, which was almost in sight.

The day had slipped away from him and darkness was falling before Clint finally pulled back on the reins. Although Fort Laramie wasn't quite in sight just yet, he knew he was getting close enough to be concerned. This was no abandoned homestead or lonely ranch he was riding to. It was a functioning military outpost manned by trained soldiers. For the moment, it didn't matter whose side they were on. Those soldiers were all a threat to Clint.

He knew the chain of command had been corrupted, and if those responsible had played their cards right, every last man in that fort would be working for them whether they knew it or not. All it took was one patrol reporting to the wrong man and Clint would be looking down several dozen government-issue firearms.

Until he knew exactly who was who, Clint wasn't about to draw on any man in uniform. Charging an army outpost was something he could live with. Accidentally killing an honest soldier was not.

After slowing Eclipse to a fast trot, Clint reached into one of his saddlebags and removed the spyglass waiting there. It took a moment or two to adjust to the jostling of the view through the glass, but soon Clint compensated for Eclipse's movement and began picking out various important sights around him.

The first of those was a two-man patrol riding around the fort's outer perimeter. From that distance and with the fading light, all Clint could see was the shapes of the horses and that the riders were wearing the regulation blue of the United States Army. Once he saw which way the patrol was headed, Clint steered for the opposite direction and moved in a bit closer to his destination.

Being careful not to skyline himself, Clint kept to the lower ground whenever possible as he rode closer to the fort. Once he got close enough to see the first couple of structures, he dismounted and led Eclipse by the reins. He didn't have to signal the Darley Arabian in the slightest to keep quiet. It was as if the stallion could feel Clint's tension for himself.

Keeping his senses on the alert for more patrols, Clint crept closer and closer to the nearby structures. He could see smoke curling into the air, and started to hear the sounds of activity and voices that were inevitable when so many people were brought together in one place. Normally, he sought out those signs as a way to lead himself to towns and such. Now, however, he used those signals as a warning.

His entire purpose was to get to Fort Laramie, but he couldn't show himself too soon. The fewer people that saw him coming, the better. Whoever was the corrupting element inside those walls was surely on the lookout as well. Clint figured he would give them as little time as possible to prepare. He knew only too well that the rider of that Appaloosa was already spreading the word about what he'd seen.

After slipping past another set of guards making their rounds on horseback, Clint climbed back into the saddle and snapped the reins. Once he'd crested the little rise that he'd been using as cover, Clint got a good look at where he'd been headed this entire time.

Fort Laramie didn't look like much at first. In fact, it resembled just another small town or possibly a large ranch. It was a collection of long, flat buildings spread out over flat, open ground. Clint couldn't even make out any walls as such, since the outer buildings were blocking his view. He didn't have any trouble spotting the soldiers, however, since they were riding up to meet him before he could get much closer.

Clint took a deep breath, held it for a second, and then let it out. He'd been doing a lot of thinking about what he would do once he got to Fort Laramie. Now that he was there, he needed to steel himself for whatever was ahead.

He'd seen more than his share of fights, and the worst ones were never judged by how many shots had been fired or how much blood had been spilled. The worst ones got that way when the men involved in them didn't know what was coming. Even fights on battlefields during times of war became especially brutal when they came from out of nowhere.

Clint wasn't exactly ignorant of what was on its way, but he didn't exactly have a clear picture either. The soldiers riding up to him could be asking to see if he had a message to deliver, or they could be ready to blast him off of Eclipse's back.

The next couple of seconds could pass just as Clint had planned, or they could mark the beginning of the end. Clint knew he was quick with the iron, but he wasn't about to fool himself into thinking he could take on a battalion of armed troops. One step in the wrong direction could be his last.

At this particular moment, Clint couldn't even say he was happy where the right direction was leading.

"You there," one of the soldiers said as they drew up to Clint and brought Eclipse to a stop. "State your name and business here."

Clint knew there was no more time to think things through. It was too late for that. All that was left for him now was to steady himself, take a deep breath, and walk straight into whatever the next moment held for him. All his planning, caution, and skill were about to pay off.

Of course, a little luck sure wouldn't hurt.

FORTY

"There's an injured man not too far from here," Clint said at a quick, panicked pace. "Someone needs to send a doctor to go tend to him."

"Who are you?" the guard asked again.

"He might be on his way back here, but he won't make it if he doesn't get help soon."

The guard's hand drifted toward his gun. The other guard riding alongside him already had his weapon ready to fire.

"This is a U.S. Army outpost," the first guard stated.

"I know. That's why I came here." Clint shook his head as though he'd suddenly recalled what had been asked of him before. "My name's John Brewster," he said, giving the name of a faro dealer he'd met the last time he was in the Carolinas. "I was passing through on business and my friend was hurt. He's south by southeast of here. You can't miss him."

"Was there an attack? How were you hurt?"

"We were robbed." Clint shrugged and added, "At least that's how it started. Some men rode by and I think they tried to rob us. Either we weren't who they thought we were, or we didn't have anything good enough to keep them happy, because they just knocked us around and rode off. One of them was hurt, though."

"One of the robbers?"

"Yeah." Clint gave a quick description of one of the other riflemen. "He and three others had rifles and asked us about some fella named Adams. Sounded like it was real important."

That caught the guards' attention. Both of them shot glances to each other and then looked back to Clint.

"What did they say exactly?" the second guard asked. "Did they have anyone else with them?"

"No. Like I said, one of them was hurt. I got the hell out of there when they moved on and came here for some help."

"If you'd like to come with us, you can show us where your friend is."

"I know you soldiers are busy, so just point me in the direction of the hospital or doc's cabin or whatever you got around here and I'll get him myself."

"We can't have you unescorted inside the perimeter, so—"

"Aw, hell, then I'll get to somewhere that can help me. I know there's a town with some law around here and I'm sure they'll want to know about those goddamn robbers."

With Clint talking so fast and him dropping the right names and adding just the right amount of urgency in his voice, he was able to get the guards flustered as well. Both of the uniformed men glanced back and forth, and then finally made a decision as to just how big a threat this John Brewster truly was.

"The hospital's over there," the guard said, pointing to a cluster of buildings away from the main section of the complex. "Go talk to the—" He was stopped by the sound of the second guard clearing his throat. Waving it off, the first guard said, "There ain't nothing else over there besides the NCO quarters anyhow. That is, unless you think he's gonna steal something from your spot."

Clint smiled and put his hand on his heart. "I'm an honest man, sir. I just need to speak to someone about getting someone to patch up my friend."

"Well, go talk to the doc and he'll see about getting someone to accompany you to your friend. In the meantime, what else did you hear those robbers say? It could help us in case we need to go out after them as well."

After pretending to think about that question for a few moments, Clint shook his head. "I can't think of a damn thing. To tell you the truth, I was just too worried about getting back to where—"

"Yeah, all right then. Go on and talk to the doc."

Although Clint appeared to be a bit rattled and confused by the sudden lack of interest coming from the guards, he couldn't have been more happy. "Uh, yes, sir. Right away, sir," he stammered while giving the two guards a sloppy salute.

The two men looked back at him with a condescending smile and went on their way. As soon as they thought they were out of earshot, they began whispering back and forth to each other about what they'd just heard.

Not only did this allow Clint to get closer to the fort, but it told him that those two men in particular could not be trusted. Responding the way they did to what Clint had said had tipped their hands as to which side of the fence they'd landed.

Clint went over all of this in his head as he rode in the direction that had been pointed out to him. The buildings in front of him were separated from what was obviously the main body of the fort. For the most part, those buildings resembled bunkhouses that could be found on a particularly big ranch. The hospital was marked with a sign, and Clint headed straight for it.

Every so often, he would take a glance over his shoulder as if he was just checking with the guards to make sure he was going the right way. The two men in uniform were watching him at first and kept waving him on. Once he got closer to the hospital, however, Clint saw the guards steer away and ride in another direction. It was plain to see that they were in a hurry to get wherever they were going.

Although there were other men moving throughout the complex, walking or riding between the buildings, they were all going about their business and paid Clint little or no mind at all. Once he was certain that the two men who were watching him before were now gone, Clint drew Eclipse to a halt and swung down from the saddle.

Clint was about ten yards from the front of the hospital. He changed direction without breaking stride and completely shed the uncertain persona he'd used to get past the guards. Instead, he straightened up and put a serious look on his face.

At the last moment, he wrapped the reins around the horn of Eclipse's saddle and gave the Darley Arabian a swat on the rump. The stallion responded perfectly to the signal and trotted off a ways to wait for Clint's signal to return.

There was still plenty of ground to cover, only this time Clint had to get as far as he could without being seen. The end was already coming. There was no need to rush it.

FORTY-ONE

One of the oldest tricks in the book when trying to hide was to do so in plain sight. That trick worked especially well when there was enough going on all around that it acted as a natural camouflage. Fort Laramie was just such a perfect place to hide out in the open. Men and women were carrying out their duties or simply going about their lives without stopping to pay any mind to yet another face that passed them by.

To discourage the few folks who might question him, Clint quickened his steps and put on an expression that was unmistakably rigid. His eyes were set firmly on the path directly in front of him, and he walked as though nothing could possibly get in his way. Most folks didn't want to get in the way of a man like that. It was a kind of natural instinct to step aside rather than be stepped on.

Clint's expression was good enough to even get him past several uniformed men who looked as if they were just about to pull him aside. But Clint wasn't stopped. Not even when he walked from the hospital and NCO quarters back to the fort's parade grounds. Just because he'd made it that far, however, didn't mean that Clint was anxious to push his luck. Before he walked in the path of someone who wasn't so easily ignored, he ducked around the closest building he could find.

That building was a longer, narrower building that gave off more noise than most of the others. Taking a quick look inside, Clint saw that he'd found what appeared to be a saloon for the enlisted men. He guessed it was so because it was too crowded and a bit too disheveled to be a place set aside for officers. Of course, the low ranks stitched onto the shoulders of the men he saw helped Clint's appraisal as well.

While he'd never worn a uniform himself, Clint had been to enough forts to recognize the similarities. He'd also been around enough army men to know what was and what wasn't acceptable when walking among them. To this end, he refrained from walking into the saloon since he knew he wouldn't make it two steps without being recognized.

Switching the expression on his face from stern and rigid to friendly and mildly dazed, Clint caught the attention of a kid who looked as if he was just barely old enough to join the military. "Excuse me," he said to the uniformed kid who seemed more than a little anxious to get into the saloon and start drinking. "Would you happen to know where I can get some boots?"

The kid looked confused and stopped just short of walking straight into the saloon. "Boots?"

"Yeah. These have a hole in them big enough to put my fist through," Clint said, jabbing a finger down toward his feet. "I could use a coat too."

The young soldier looked Clint up and down before telling him, "This isn't a trading post."

"Where did you get your boots?"

"From the quartermaster, but that's only for army men."

Clint paused for a moment and narrowed his eyes slightly. When he spoke again, the civility was gone from his voice, leaving the vocal equivalent to a sheet of ice. "What's your name, soldier?"

"My name?"

"I'd like to know it so I can come back here once I get the supplies I'm after so you can see my uniform for yourself." Clint could see other men walking toward him out of the corner of his eye. He didn't let that affect him, however, and kept his posture and voice rigid.

Clint's patience paid off. The bluff was working. That much was evident by the increasing level of panic on the young soldier's face. "I didn't know, sir," he replied, straightening up. "Should I . . . uhh . . . salute you?"

"You can tell me where the quartermaster is," Clint said. "Worry about saluting the next time you see me."

"Right that way, uh, sir." The soldier pointed across the parade grounds, and when Clint looked back at him, he saluted crisply.

"At ease," Clint said before turning and walking toward the building the soldier had pointed out. Even though he knew he had the young uniformed man cowed well enough, Clint didn't relax until he heard the man enter the saloon. Just to be safe, he quickened his pace before the soldier could point him out to any of his friends inside.

That walk across the parade grounds seemed to take all day.

Every step of the way, Clint was certain someone would spot him and recognize who he was. At the very least, he was convinced that someone would know he didn't belong and would bring him in to talk to a man who truly did wear stripes on his shoulders.

Normally, Clint had nothing but respect for men in uniform. This time was different, however. This time, he knew for a fact that plenty of uniformed men around him were wolves hiding among the sheep. Until the time came to bare his own fangs, Clint was forced to be another sheep.

He didn't like that one bit, and the knot in his stomach didn't unravel until he made it to the wide, flat building and pulled open the door. There was just a sign hanging outside the door that marked the building as the quartermaster's. It was triple the size of a large stable and wider than two normal storefronts. That made it seem all the stranger when Clint walked inside to find himself in a space that reminded him of a modest hotel's lobby.

With walls on either side as well as in front of him, Clint felt as if he'd somehow walked into the wrong place. But the echo of his footsteps affirmed the size of the building. The walls had been put there to section out a small waiting area from where all the supplies were kept. Directly in front of Clint was a window cut through the dividing wall. That window was barred and there were shutters closed behind the bars.

Clint walked up to the window and knocked on the wall beside it. He didn't have to wait long before hearing footsteps approach the window and seeing the shutters pulled open.

"Hello," Clint said casually. "I'm looking for Master Sergeant Mortenson."

The man on the other side of the bars smiled and nodded. "That'd be me."

"I'm—"

"You're Clint Adams," the man behind the bars said. "I know. We've been expecting you." That last statement was punctuated by the unmistakable click of a pistol's hammer cocking into firing position.

FORTY-TWO

With the click of that hammer still sounding through the air, Clint could also hear heavy steps thumping against the boards just outside the door behind him. In moments, the door leading outside was opened and uniformed men started flowing inside.

Not one of the faces were familiar, but Clint had a good idea that those were all the very men he'd been looking for. The ranks of the soldiers ranged from enlisted men to officers, but that was just according to what was on their clothes. Clint was certain that the men inside those clothes had done nothing to earn their ranks.

Once the waiting room was lined with uniformed men, the only exit was closed and Clint was left staring into the amused eyes of the man behind the bars.

"I'll be damned," the man wearing Ken Mortenson's uniform said. "I knew you'd be a problem from the moment I heard about you becoming a lawman in Duskin, but I thought for certain you'd be happy to stay in your little town and keep running drunks into jail."

Shrugging, Clint replied, "And I might have been if one of you hadn't gunned someone down right in front of me."

"Well, that's where you first started surprising us,

Adams. You weren't even supposed to walk away from that platform."

Clint thought back to that day, which seemed so very long ago. Even now, it all blended together, but he could still pick out the face of the man he'd killed from his memory. That face was right along with all the others that he'd killed. It haunted him, just as it would any man who happened to have a conscience.

"Come to think of it, that fella did seem pretty surprised," Clint said. "That surprise was on his face even when I dropped him with one shot."

Suddenly, Clint felt a hand slap against his shoulder from behind.

"I rode with that man through hell and back, asshole," came a voice from behind Clint. "And I'm not about to stand by and let you—"

Having successfully forced someone's hand, Clint reacted without letting another second go by. First off, his hand clamped down over the hand that was already on his shoulder. From there, he turned and dropped to one knee. That motion not only forced the man's wrist and arm to bend the wrong way, but it twisted him around and kept him from moving an inch as Clint took some control back from the situation.

When he came to a stop, Clint just had to take part of a step to put himself right up against the man who'd stepped up to say his piece. Although all of the uniformed men had been expecting Clint to draw his gun, not one of them was fast enough to keep him from doing it. Before any of them could say a word or make another move, Clint's modified Colt had cleared leather.

Having started out full of bluster, the man who'd reached out to grab Clint's shoulder now found that the tables had turned in every possible way. Not only was he completely at Clint's mercy, but he wasn't able to say another word.

"I didn't come all this way just to stroll into a trap," Clint said, pressing the Colt's barrel against the side of the man's head directly in front of him. "And before any of you get any ideas, just know that even if your shot does hit me, it'll more than likely go right through and kill this one here as well."

Everyone else in the room looked over to the man who was still standing behind the bars. That man nodded before too long, which caused all of them to lower their guns.

"That's the best you're gonna get for now, Adams," the man said.

Frankly, that was more than Clint expected. He must have lucked out and gotten hold of someone important.

"All right then," Clint said. "How about I get a look at what's in this building."

The man behind the bars nodded and started pulling latches on his side of the wall. "You're welcome to it. In fact, I was gonna give you a look anyhow, so you could just go ahead and let that one go. From what I hear, you're not the type to hide behind a hostage."

"I'm not. But this isn't exactly a situation where I've got much choice." Even so, Clint relaxed his grip and allowed the man he'd been holding to step away.

After pulling open a section of the wall beside the bars, the man behind them revealed a door that had been flush with the rest of the partition. He was nodding slowly when he said, "I knew you had more honor than most."

Clint kept his eyes and body moving so he could keep tabs on everyone around him. "I've just already seen what your men have and know I can gun any of them down before the rest could lift their arms."

From anyone else, that statement would have seemed like the bragging of an overconfident man. From Clint Adams, however, the words were pure fact, and everyone else in that room accepted them as such.

"Tell you what, Adams," the man in Mortenson's uniform said. "As a show of good faith, I'll have these others hold back here for the moment. I'd like to have a word with you before this whole thing gets out of hand."

"Out of hand? I'd say it's way past that already."

"But it doesn't have to get any farther. Come on and have your look around. We won't be bothered by anyone else."

As he said that, there came another sound from outside the building. It was the voice of a bugle being played in a quick, sharp melody. Clint may not have been a soldier, but he knew a battlefield call when he heard one. Even though he'd heard a few of those before, he'd never heard anything like this one.

"That's a cadence to make sure we have some privacy, Adams. Take my word for it. That this whole building could burn down before any unwanted visitors poke their noses around here."

Clint stepped through the door and pulled it shut behind him. He fastened whatever latches he could find, and figured that would keep most of those others in that smaller room for a little while. When he turned his eyes to the large, open room on the other side of those bars, his eyes widened and his jaw almost hit the floor.

"Jesus Christ," Clint whispered. "I'm too late."

FORTY-THREE

For all practical purposes, the building that was supposed to contain supplies and weapons for Fort Laramie was cleaned out. There were stacks of crates here and there as well as a few odd piles of sacks and clothing, but those things seemed to be rattling around within so much empty space that Clint felt like he'd stepped into a ghost town.

He and the other man walked through the space until Clint could get a look into the section set aside as the armory. Although there wasn't quite as much empty space there, that was only because the room itself was smaller.

"I brought you here to make you an offer," the uniformed man said.

Clint put on his poker face and looked over to him. "I don't deal with men I don't know."

The man smirked and shook his head. "And you don't need to know me unless we're partners. But before you get too set in your ways, just hear me out."

"Go on." Even though he said that, Clint wanted to use whatever time he could get to think things through and hopefully come up with what to do next.

"This whole room used to be full. The man who wore this uniform used to keep it that way. It was his job, but it didn't pay well because he was handing this merchandise out to the wrong people."

"If you wanted to open a store," Clint said, "there's much safer ways to go about it."

"True, but that's only if I wanted to open just any old store. Do you know how much money certain people are willing to pay for supplies that the army takes for granted? I do, and it's a small fortune."

"I'll bet. Especially when you want to sell stolen weapons and ammunition."

"And don't forget the uniforms. Genuine army uniforms go for a pretty penny when you sell to the right people."

"People like robbers or fugitives?" Clint replied.

The man finished that statement without hesitation. "Or assassins. They pay quite handsomely. Look, I'd only be insulting your intelligence and wasting both our time if I tried to make this look like anything other than what it is. I'm not trying to hide what's going on. I'm trying to cut you in on it."

"Why?"

"Because we could use a man like you."

"And who's 'we'?"

"We're no different than any other company, only we just happen to work on the other side of the law than most. We're not the first to organize and we won't be the last. You can either profit from finding us or die. It's your choice."

"What about Ken Mortenson?" Clint asked. "Did you give him the same choice?"

The man looked down at the uniform he was wearing and shrugged. "I did, and he made the wrong one."

"What about those people you were trying to kill on that platform? What about Larry Brunell? Did you give them the same choice?"

"You know what happened to them, Adams, and I don't think I like where this is headed. I'd much rather make you rich along with the rest of us than start something that won't end after a whole lot of blood is spilled."

"Make me rich?" Clint scoffed. "How would that happen? By selling guns and army outfits to bandits trying to change their identity and killers looking to slip past a few lawmen?"

The man cocked his head as if he didn't know quite how to take what Clint was saying. Although he was still conflicted, he stepped over to a small desk that still had Master Sergeant Mortenson's nameplate on it. "Take a look at this," he said, picking up a leather-bound book and tossing it over to Clint. "I bet you'll recognize some of those names, and I sure as hell know you'll recognize the size of those payments they're making to get what I have to sell."

Clint opened the book and flipped through some of the pages. He didn't have to pretend to be impressed with some of the names he found there. Not only were some of them well-known criminals and politicians, but some of them had been hiding so well for so long that they'd been assumed to be dead.

"With what I know and the people I've been recruiting," the man said, "we'll have enough firepower to sell to be rich several times over. There are other forts and other sources of guns. There's enough for us to spread thunder across every inch of this country."

"Yeah. I don't doubt that."

"Then what do you say, Adams? Do you want to be a rich man? We sure could use a man of your talents."

Clint closed the book, but did not hand it over. "Being rich is too complicated. I'd rather settle for other things like being able to sleep at night or look at myself in a mirror."

"Come on now. There's not one businessman alive who didn't do some things he's ashamed of. Hell, even the regular folks have some crosses to bear. What about that lovely little sister back in Duskin?"

"Who are you talking about?"

The man motioned toward his uniform and smirked again. "You don't think she really just happened to bump into you? And you may be a lady killer, but you've got to admit that she kept you plenty busy while Ed was across the way doing his own job."

What disturbed Clint the most about all of that was that it seemed to make perfect sense. "Either way, that job didn't get done well enough. I'm here and I know all about what's going on. And thanks to you, I know more. Whatever your name is, your business is finished."

The man took a breath and nodded slowly. "And here I thought I could count on you to at least go along with us for a while. Maybe just try to get in close and get to know everyone a bit more?"

"Why would I want to do that?" Clint asked. "Whatever I haven't already found out, I can get from this book."

"Ah, well, that's true. Of course there's just one little catch to that. You're going to have to make it out of here alive."

FORTY-FOUR

Clint's eyes were focused on the man in front of him, waiting for any sign of him going for his gun or any other movement. Instead, the man simply took a breath and let it out in the form of a piercing whistle that could have been used to call in the horses from the opposite end of a ranch.

The floor shook with the impact of all those boots rushing in from the smaller outer room. There was also the rattling of side doors being thrown open as men streamed in from every angle, every last one of them converging on Clint's position.

As this was happening, Clint tightened his grip on the book and moved to put his back against some solid cover. That was the moment that he was given the very thing he'd been waiting for. The man who'd been doing all the talking while wearing a dead man's uniform started bringing his pistol up to fire.

Clint's hand flashed toward his Colt, which seemed to be the signal for all of hell to break loose.

Drawing the modified weapon, Clint aimed and squeezed his trigger, causing the man in Ken Mortenson's uniform to spin like a top and fall over spouting blood from his wound. Thinking about what he'd just heard made it difficult for Clint to adjust his aim, but he managed to do so in time. The other man was hurt, but alive for the moment.

All around him, Clint heard gunshots explode through the air and echo within the walls of the nearly empty building. Even with all those men trying to kill him, however, there seemed to be more gunshots than what he would have expected. The thunder of pistol fire roared inside and outside the building, putting Clint once again in the middle of a leaden storm.

Clint's mind worked at double speed, which still didn't seem fast enough considering what was happening. Everywhere he looked, there was another man taking a shot at him. When he saw an opening for a clean shot, Clint didn't hesitate to take it. By now, even the sight of the blue federal uniforms wasn't slowing him down.

The modified Colt bucked in Clint's hand, spitting out another round and delivering another man to the grave. Before that man hit the floor, there was another one to take his place, and it was all Clint could do to keep moving before getting hit himself.

Throwing himself forward, Clint reached out with both hands while launching off of both feet. He flew through the air, only to be caught by his outstretched arms so he could land in a tight, rolling ball. He stopped himself with one leg shot out to the side and focused his eyes just in time to see a pair of soldiers running toward him with murder in their eyes.

Despite the chaos, Clint's mind automatically ticked off the number of shots that he'd fired. He knew there was only one live bullet left in his cylinder, so he rolled a few feet to the right to line up his shot. When he came to a stop this time, the two men that were running at him were in a row. Clint lifted the Colt, aimed carefully, and squeezed his trigger.

The bullet whipped through the air at a slightly upward angle. It drilled a hole through the front man's neck and punched directly into the face of the man behind him. Both attackers dropped and their eyeballs rolled up into their heads. Their guns went off at the behest of fists clenching only in the first, twitching moments of death.

Now that he was closer to one of the outer walls of the building, Clint could hear more of what was going on outside. He listened while reloading the Colt, and by the time he snapped the cylinder shut, he knew there was definitely another battle being fought out there. He didn't know who was doing the fighting, but he was sure glad that some of the heat was being pulled away from him.

Clint could feel the others nearby, but couldn't see so many of them since the gunmen were now seeking cover. A quick survey of his surroundings told Clint that the closest exit was about fifteen yards away. Pulling in a deep breath, Clint held his Colt at the ready and prepared to make a run for it.

It was going to be risky.

It might have been a stupid risk.

It might have even been impossible.

While Clint knew all of those things, he also knew that his odds weren't going to get any better if he just waited around in that same spot. So, with the book still clutched under his left arm, he held his head low and charged out from where he'd been hiding.

When he started running, Clint felt as well as heard the gunshots that followed. It seemed as though the air itself had exploded, and there was nothing for him to do except keep running through the flames.

Just as Clint started picking up speed, he spotted the man in Ken Mortenson's uniform pulling himself up onto his feet. There were other men closing in on him as well from either side, so Clint shifted the Colt's aim accordingly.

When the men next to Mortenson's replacement saw Clint, they made the fatal mistake of taking aim at the oncoming figure. Clint responded by aiming as though he

was just pointing at first one and then the other. In that order, the two men dropped as bullets from the Colt's smoking mouth burned them down.

The man in Mortenson's uniform was stunned by the
sudden death of his two guards, but not nearly as stunned
as he was when Clint practically yanked him from his
boots as he came running by. The wind was knocked from
his lungs on impact and by the time he got it back, he was
already headed for the exit.

Clint carried the imposter with him almost as though he
was dragging a child. The other man was resisting, but
Clint was too strong, too worked up, and had too much momentum to be beaten. In no time at all, both men were
through the door and out of the building.

Unfortunately, Clint found himself leaving one skir-
mish just so he could run face-first onto a battlefield.

FORTY-FIVE

For a moment, Clint thought he'd stepped straight into a nightmare. There were so many blue uniforms out there that he knew he couldn't fight through them all. Fortunately, he quickly saw that not all of those uniforms were wolves in sheep's clothing. In fact, a good number of them were genuine soldiers fighting against the imposters. It didn't take long for Clint to figure out who'd turned the tide.

"Hey, Adams! You didn't think I'd just sit back and let you have all the fun, did you?"

The sight of Sam Wise riding beside an older uniformed army officer was the proverbial sight for Clint's sore eyes. Keeping low while the shooting went on around him, Clint headed to where Sam was and dragged his human cargo right along with him.

"What brings you here?" Clint asked once he was close enough. "Not that I mind, of course."

Sam took aim with the rifle he was holding, and dropped the hammer on one of the killers who'd been following Clint out from the quartermaster's building. "I knew you'd be headed for Cheyenne and here," he said through the smoke. "So I figured I'd try to do what I could to help. I

180

smoothed the way for you in Cheyenne, and stopped by here myself once I was able."

"How'd you know to come here first?"

"It was closer."

"Good enough for me. Who's this?"

Turning to the army man on the horse beside his, Sam said, "This is Colonel Randolph Gray. He was staying at a hotel in town and I asked him if he was interested in a little ride."

The colonel tipped his hat and said, "I could tell things were odd here at first sight. The rest was just a matter of rounding up the men and taking a look for ourselves."

Although there were still some pops of gunfire here and there, most of it was tapering off. By the looks of it, once they could no longer hide, the imposters who could still move were turning tail and running. A few more charged from the building, but the first wave was gunned down by Clint, Sam, and the colonel. After that, the men came out slowly and with their hands held high.

Colonel Gray gave the order to his men for prisoners to be rounded up. With Clint's help, the soldiers knew where to look, and quickly gathered the imposters outside of the quartermaster's building.

"Here, Colonel," Clint said, holding out a folded piece of paper he'd taken from his inner jacket pocket. "This is a list of the names of army men who might either be missing, dead, or a part of this group."

The colonel took the list and shook his head. "Nothing I hate more than a bunch of war profiteers. I'll see to it personally that every one of these men are accounted for. Thank you, Mr. Adams." With that, the colonel rode off to supervise the rest of the cleanup.

Clint waited for Sam to climb down from his horse so he could speak in a lower tone of voice. "I'm sure that colonel is a good man, but I'd rather hand this over to you all the same." Clint gave Sam the leather-bound book. "The men in there are this one's clients," he said, nodding toward the imposter standing nearby.

The man in Mortenson's uniform was beaten and he knew it. The time for running was long gone, so he just stood in his place and stared daggers at everyone around him.

"I think Anne Mortenson may be a part of this," Clint said. Glaring at the imposter, he asked, "Is that true, or was that just another crock of lies?"

"I didn't lie to you, Adams," the uniformed wolf said. "There's no need for it."

"I'll look in on her," Sam said. "With all this information to use, I can either trip her up or clear her name pretty quickly."

"You're a hell of a lawman, Sam," Clint said, offering his hand.

Shaking Clint's hand, Sam nodded. "Only because of having partners like you to work with."

"Do me one more favor."

"Name it, Clint."

"Send a message onto the U.S. marshals telling them what and who is in that book."

"I've got some names. But you could always do it yourself, Clint. You're more than welcome to come back to Duskin and keep the peace. If you'll let me pay you what you're worth, you could make a hell of a life for yourself."

Clint spotted a familiar figure in the distance, whistled to it, and watched as Eclipse rode up to get him. "Thanks, Sam, but I've already got a hell of a life. It's time for me to get back to it."

With that, Clint climbed into the saddle and rode through the dozens of army men rounding up the straggling imposters. He rode away from Fort Laramie, away from Duskin and away from Wyoming.

Away was all that mattered.

The only storm he wanted a part of was the rolling thunder of Eclipse's hooves and the wind rushing past his ears.

Watch for

THE HANGING JUDGE

278th novel in the exciting GUNSMITH
series from Jove

Coming in February!

J. R. ROBERTS

THE GUNSMITH

Explore the exciting Old West with one of the men who made it wild!

AVAILABLE WHEREVER BOOKS ARE SOLD OR AT
WWW.PENGUIN.COM

(Ad # B112)